CASTLEDAWN

CASTLEDAWN

RAYMOND MOORE

For my sister Angela

First published in 2023 by Redshank Books

Redshank Books is an imprint of Libri Publishing.

Copyright © Raymond Moore

The right of Raymond Moore to be identified as the author of this work has been asserted in accordance with the Copyright, Designs and Patents Act, 1988.

ISBN 978-1-912969-59-3

All rights reserved. No part of this publication may be reproduced, stored in any retrieval system or transmitted in any form or by any means, electronic, mechanical, photocopying, recording or otherwise, without the prior written permission of the copyright holder for which application should be addressed in the first instance to the publishers. No liability shall be attached to the author, the copyright holder or the publishers for loss or damage of any nature suffered as a result of reliance on the reproduction of any of the contents of this publication or any errors or omissions in its contents.

A CIP catalogue record for this book is available from The British Library

Cover and book design by Carnegie Book Production

Libri Publishing
Brunel House
Volunteer Way
Faringdon
Oxfordshire
SN7 7YR

Tel: +44 (0)845 873 3837

www.libripublishing.co.uk

CASTLEDAWN

RAYMOND MOORE

For my sister Angela

First published in 2023 by Redshank Books

Redshank Books is an imprint of Libri Publishing.

Copyright © Raymond Moore

The right of Raymond Moore to be identified as the author of this work has been asserted in accordance with the Copyright, Designs and Patents Act, 1988.

ISBN 978-1-912969-59-3

All rights reserved. No part of this publication may be reproduced, stored in any retrieval system or transmitted in any form or by any means, electronic, mechanical, photocopying, recording or otherwise, without the prior written permission of the copyright holder for which application should be addressed in the first instance to the publishers. No liability shall be attached to the author, the copyright holder or the publishers for loss or damage of any nature suffered as a result of reliance on the reproduction of any of the contents of this publication or any errors or omissions in its contents.

A CIP catalogue record for this book is available from The British Library

Cover and book design by Carnegie Book Production

Libri Publishing
Brunel House
Volunteer Way
Faringdon
Oxfordshire
SN7 7YR

Tel: +44 (0)845 873 3837

www.libripublishing.co.uk

PROLOGUE

The Isle of Skye 1855

It was a miserable winter afternoon; the sun had not broken through the gloomy grey clouds all day and now it was sinking behind the Uists. Seven-year-old Donald Angus Macpherson guessed he had half an hour of daylight left, maybe more, to roam the rocky shore of Score Bay in his search for whelks. His mother had sent him to feed the hens – but the attraction of the sea and treasure on the shore was impossible to ignore. With his wee grey metal bucket in hand, he walked towards the Minch.

Hidden in the shadow of the Duntulm Castle cliff – he knew where to find the biggest black shelled beasties. The tide was on the turn, and the black, cold sea edged closer as he climbed the huge, jagged rock that was home to the biggest whelks in the North End. Incoming waves snaked frothy and frigid around his welly wearing feet– ten more minutes he thought.

From Harris a blustery wind rolled across the water towards Duntulm bringing sheets of sidewinder rain. Above the black house where Donald lived – a thin wisp of peaty smoke squiggled through the air. Inside was rare and warm – a roaring fire awaited his return.

Winter dark fast approached, and he'd neglected to bring a jacket to protect him from the incoming deluge – five more minutes, just five. What light was left faded and big, bulbous raindrops landed on his head and hands – two more minutes.

On page two of the Inverness Courier, it was reported that on the 10th of November a seven-year-old boy had gone missing in North Skye. D.A. Macpherson was last seen by his mother in the late afternoon when he had gone to feed the chickens. The boy frequented the shore at Duntulm, and it was suggested he could have drowned – a search of the beach and the surrounding area had turned up nothing.

It was also noted that Donald Angus was the third boy to go missing locally in the past year. Police inquiries were ongoing.

CHAPTER 1

Stepping off the school bus, Donald John McKay wore a mile-wide smile – school was definitely out, and the summer holidays could finally begin. Ahead of him lay two months of fun and mischief making with his two Totescore pals – brothers James and John Macdonald. A big sun lumbered west, and the township basked in its yellow glow. A breeze rolled down from the Linicro hill, carrying the scent of foxglove and heather.

With a push and a kick, he opened the big wooden gate in front of his house, the old shepherd's cottage. He called on Bess, the family Collie, who ran towards him, all black and white wagging tail. She barked and dog-smiled as if greeting a long-lost friend – DJ had last seen her in the morning before leaving for school, but the dog had missed her pal and wanted to show him some love. Sitting outside the front door was Catriona, DJ's four-year-old sister, playing with a headless Barbie doll – Bess had recently decapitated it and poor Barbie, with her long blonde locks had been mauled beyond recognition. His sister talked to the doll as if it was a living, breathing person – a living, breathing person with no head that is. When it happened, the murder of Barbie by Bess was a heinous crime and Catriona cried and cried, but she soon recovered from her grief with the help of a Penguin chocolate biscuit and a kiss from her mum.

"Hi Catriona, how's Barbie's headache," DJ smiled, his hand ruffling her wavy hair.

"Barbie's head gone," she replied, not looking up.

Entering the cottage, DJ's nose was greeted by the familiar and comforting smell of freshly baked treacle scones. The aroma hung head height and his stomach rumbled in appreciation. His mum was in the back kitchen, so he shouted, "I'm back," before climbing the steep wooden steps to his bedroom. Hanging his Portree High School blazer in the closet, he closed the creaky door, flipping its rusty hook into a metal fencing staple – happy in the knowledge he wouldn't be wearing it for two months. He threw the rest of his school clothes into a yellow plastic laundry bin. Time to change into his summer uniform – a white t-shirt, Wrangler jeans and a pair of black and white Gola trainers.

"DJ, DJ. We need water please!" called his mum from below. Though not quite an order, he knew if he delayed the tone would change, and it would become an order to be obeyed immediately. Half jumping down the steps he made his way to the kitchen, and to his mum, who tried to kiss him and almost succeeded.

"How was your last day darling?"

"OK."

"And?"

"It was good."

His mum knew she wouldn't get much more out of him and pointed to the two empty blue plastic buckets on the kitchen table – no other words were needed. The cottage didn't have running water, so they relied on a stream that bubbled up from the ground and ran through their croft not far from the house. The stream, known locally as the tobar – which was Gaelic for 'a well,' – had served fresh, clean, cold water to generations of Linicro folk. He grabbed the buckets and headed out the back door. At times he hated this chore, but it remained a magical mystery to him, and he often wondered about the source of the water. From high on the hill, it ran underground until it emerged from what looked like a miniature cave – fast flowing and always clear as crystal. Long dead crofters had placed two steadfast rocks either side of the well mouth, enabling feet to stand as the water rushed through outstretched legs. DJ cleaned the area of weeds and spiders' webs at least once a week, and it was rare that anything other than pure fresh water got into his buckets. Crouching, he tipped each bucket on its side and let the water rush in until both were brim full. He'd been carrying water buckets back and forth every day since they arrived in Linicro and noticed the strength in his arms had increased – biceps had appeared, muscles he didn't have when he lived in the city. He placed the buckets back on the kitchen table, the flowery waxed tablecloth preventing the inevitable water spills from penetrating the wood and causing wood rot. Hanging on the wall above the table was a shining aluminium measuring jug – used for scooping water from the buckets into thirsty mouths and for filling kettles and pots.

DJ hadn't always lived in Linicro – just over a year ago his mum had moved him and his sister from a spacious three bedroomed flat in the Bruntsfield area of Edinburgh. Their lives had changed two years previous when his dad dropped dead at work. An aneurysm they called it – could've had it for years the Doctor told his mum. DJ's mum was a nurse and knew that most folk had no symptoms, most folk looked fit and well until the day their aneurysm ruptured. His dad was only thirty-five years old and to DJ it seemed like it had happened yesterday – it also seemed like it had happened a long time ago.

For months after the funeral, DJ would sit in the kitchen, waiting for his dad to return from the school where he taught English – he never did come home. His mum kept everything together, ensuring life carried on as normal as possible for DJ and Catriona, but it would never be normal again and sometimes, at night, in the kitchen, when she was doing the ironing, he could hear her cry – had seen her cry once too, she blamed the tears on the steam from the iron.

His mum was from Liberton, his dad was from Fort William, and they met at a friend's birthday party – both students, from then until the day he died they were never apart. It was her idea to make the move to Skye. The summer before starting her nurse training, she'd worked at the Flodigarry Hotel in the north of the island and always talked about how beautiful it was and how nice it would be to live there. She saw it as a fresh start for the three of them. DJ took some convincing, though. Leaving the city and his pals wasn't easy, he cried, but not in front of her. He understood with his dad gone his mum found it hard living in the flat, what with all their shared memories and stuff. If he'd put his foot down about wanting to stay in Edinburgh – she would've agreed but he wanted to see her happy again and thought Skye might provide that happiness. DJ's mum never spoke to him like he was a child. She talked to him the same way she talked to adults. Maybe it was the nurse in her? Who knows? DJ liked it – made him feel grown up. Having said that, when she needed to, she'd give him a telling off – she was a mum, after all.

With the money from his dad's life insurance, they bought the cottage in Linicro. His mum didn't see the house beforehand – she fell in love with the photos in the estate agent's brochure. She discussed it first with DJ, smiling when she told him it lacked certain amenities, like no running water, no bath or even a toilet. The place had not been lived in since the nineteen fifties, when it housed the Linicro shepherd and his family. She called it a fixer upper – an adventure. DJ wasn't so sure, but he saw how happy she looked talking about it, that's what convinced him, her smile. They wouldn't sell the Bruntsfield flat – she'd rent it to students and if she found a part-time job, they'd have enough money to make a go of it. DJ finished primary seven in Edinburgh, and they moved to Skye in the summer of nineteen seventy-six.

Talk about culture shock – the cottage didn't even have a phone… Or worse – a telly. The house was a total mess when they arrived – they spent the whole summer cleaning the mountains of stoor that had gathered on the furniture left by the previous occupants. Some of it they kept – most of it was burned in a bonfire behind the cottage.

Norman and Maggie from the neighbouring croft were incredibly friendly and welcoming – Skye folk through and through, who helped get the cottage cleared and cleaned. Norman was as strong as a bull and did all the heavy lifting, DJ helped. Having seen the last of their children leave for university, they took the new neighbours under their wing. DJ's mum called them a Godsend – he could only agree. Between the four of them they had done a pretty good job of making the place a cosy, if compact home. At least the downstairs had electricity and there was a promise of indoor plumbing to come.

Children are resilient and even though he missed his dad madly – it took only a couple of weeks for DJ to fall in love with Linicro and his new house.

Recently, his mum had taken a part-time Staff Nurse job at Portree Hospital working two early shifts during the week and one late shift at the weekend. Catriona attended nursery at Kilmuir primary school and at the weekend DJ, with the help of Maggie did the babysitting. Most of the time Catriona was with Maggie and DJ was with his pals James and John who lived in Totescore. Their house faced the shepherd's cottage but was a couple of fields away. James was the same age as DJ, John two years older. They met on the school bus last year and the three of them became fast friends. Maggie and quite a few other crofters called them the township tearaways. They were always up for an adventure and a bit of fun.

"Are you hungry, darling?" asked his mum.

"Starving."

He scooped up some cold water and slurped it down.

"Dinner will be ready in half an hour. Keep an eye Catriona for me, please."

With a sigh, and an eye roll he left his mum to it and went out front. Under the living room window was an old railway sleeper, propped up on two large logs – his mum's attempt at a garden seat, he sat there and watched Catriona and her headless Barbie play – Bess, at his feet, watched them both.

The cottage was small, with white-washed, stone walls and a burnt orange corrugated iron roof. On the ground floor was a modest living room with a fireplace, a bedroom and at the back, a tiny kitchen. DJ's mum and sister slept in the ground floor bedroom. Upstairs there were two tiny bedrooms with sloping ceilings and tongue and groove wooden panels covering the walls. Light came through a rusty iron framed skylight window. Upstairs was accessed by a set of very steep steps, almost like a ladder. One room they used for storage and the other, above the living room was DJ's. The cottage sat on a small croft which was blanketed in ferns and thistles. An old bothy sat roofless and ruined just above the tobar. His mum planned to fix it up and talked about getting a goat or two. Catriona liked the sound of that but DJ knew if the goats materialised, he would be the one doing most of the work to look after them – could be fun though, maybe.

On one side of the house was a hen house, clad in rusty red corrugated iron sheets. They kept nine hens and a cockerel – who thought he owned the place. DJ's chores included feeding the hens, mucking out the hen house and searching the croft for hidden nests. Most of the hens laid in the henhouse but a couple liked to wander the croft and find a nice wee spot amongst the ferns to lay. At the back of the house, near the kitchen door stood two wooden sheds, one housed a chemical loo – the other an assortment of ancient looking tools.

When they first arrived, the cottage was surrounded by overgrown grass and stinging nettles. Norman brought over his razor-sharp scythe and soon got rid of all the unwanted greenery. Now, at the front of the house were two bumpy lawn patches, a couple of flowery bushes stood either side of the gate. Keeping the lawn mown was another of DJ's chores and definitely not one of his favourites. Norman had given them a push-pull lawn mower and once a week DJ could be seen pushing and pulling – all red faced and sweating. After, he raked the grass and cleaned and oiled the mower blades. His dream was to have a Flymo like Norman's, it'd have the grass and weeds under control in no time – would be fun to use, too. One day, one day he would suggest it to his mum.

On the other side of the single-track road, facing the cottage was an old blacksmiths workshop, known locally as the smiddy. Long left to wrack and ruin, its sad rusty roof had several holes, and the front door was blocked by a jungle of weeds and head height purple thistles. DJ, James, and John used it as a den – his mum wasn't happy about this, she thought it was unsafe and that the bulging gable walls were in danger of collapse – but this didn't stop the Linicro tearaways. To enter, the boys crept through the back window – it was a tight squeeze, but they managed – the wooden frame and glass panes had long surrendered to time. They had reclaimed three logs, which they used as seats under the part of the roof with the least amount of holes.

Light bars filtered through the holey roof, infused with dust particles and pollen – the wind blew through the window, allowing the air to circulate, especially welcome on hot days. The smiddy's earth floor was springy when dry and spongy when wet. Against the walls were a couple of wooden work benches – half eaten by woodworm and crumbling. Old and rusting blacksmithing tools lay scattered across the benches – on the walls, hanging from thick iron nails, was a collection of horseshoes, big and small. The boys had cleared the place of weeds and rubbish but had left the blacksmith's anvil, indestructible and heavy, they called it their den's centrepiece. The furnace remained intact and during the winter, they would light a wee fire to keep them warm. There was a radio donated by the brothers' older sister Janet which hung from a long red nail on the wall. It was tuned to Radio One medium wave and the reception wasn't the best, but crackling top twenty songs was better than no top twenty songs – and anything was better than listening to Radio Scotland.

From the smiddy's window you could see the brothers' house at the end of the Totescore road. Totescore had two single-track roads – they lived on the first. The other was a wee bit further up on the way towards Uig. You could cut across the hay fields to their house, but it took a brave soul to traverse the bogs at the bottom of the croft – a boy could easily get stuck and lose a welly or a trainer, better to bike it – which is what James and John mostly did.

The shepherd's cottage was no 2 in Linicro. No 1 belonged to old Miss Murchison – a spinster who had taken a bit of a shine to DJ and absolutely loved Catriona.

DJ often did odd jobs for the cailleach*, and the money earned he saved towards buying a new bike.

With a blade of grass in his mouth he sat, one eye on Catriona the other looking towards the Minch. The MV Hebrides was returning to Uig from Stornoway – no matter how many times, he never tired of watching the ferry coming and going. One day he promised himself – he'd sail on it.

"Dinner!" called his mum – jolting him from his ferry daydream.

"Come on Catriona, Bess. Let's get something to eat," he said.

Bess's ears pricked at the mere suggestion of food – with his sister's hand in his, DJ walked her to her highchair on the corner of the wee table in the living room. The radio was on and tuned to Radio Scotland.

"Wipe your sister's face and hands please and don't forget your own," called his mum from the kitchen.

"You want me to wipe my face?'

"Don't be cheeky, DJ" said his mum, smiling and carrying food to the table.

"Face. DJ's face. Wash," laughed Catriona.

Tonight's meal was corned beef with boiled potatoes, and baby carrots. DJ cut up Catriona's food and attempted to feed her – she wasn't particularly cooperative, more interested in feeding the beef to Bess who sat beneath her feet. The dog was smart – she knew there would be food coming from Catriona's plate.

"So... Summer holidays, exciting. What are your big plans?' asked his mum.

---

* An old woman.

"Och... You know... Just hanging out with the boys. Bike runs stuff like that," he replied.

"Just because you are on holiday doesn't mean you get a holiday from your chores," she smiled.

"Aye... I know... Don't worry mum, I'll get them done. I'm hoping Miss Murchison has some work for me. I'm getting close to the amount I need for my new bike."

"I'm sure she will have plenty for you to do, darling," she said reaching over and stroking his cheek.

Chapter 2

Candlelight illuminated DJ's bedroom; dark flame shadows danced on the sloping ceilings. Upstairs had no electricity and he read his comics by the light of a candle on his homemade bedside table – a wooden tea crate left by the previous occupants, turned upside down. If his torch had batteries, he would balance it on his shoulder, the beam focused on his comic – either The Sparky, Victor or Commando. He'd just finished the last of the Commandos he shared with James and John and was staring at the ceiling – thinking about the holiday activities he'd planned with the boys. There would be plenty of walks on the hill, along the common grazing, in the shadow of the Linicro rocks. The sheep shearing fank nearby was a massive playground for them and when the township's sheep were gathered for their annual haircut, they would be there helping the crofters. The peat road and the path above Linicro rocks was a great place to play as was the Totescore quarry where they could muck around, hidden from adult eyes. No doubt they would make a few bike trips to Uig bakery and the pier to fish with their homemade lines. The thing that excited him the most was their camping trips. The boys' older brother Duncan had picked up a green canvas army tent in a second-hand shop in Dingwall and the three of them planned to make good use of it over the coming eight weeks. DJ had talked to his mum about camping and in principle she'd agreed – as long as they didn't stray too far from the house. Linicro wasn't the city, he reminded her. Skye was safe and she didn't have to worry, the three of them were big enough to look after each other. She nodded her head in agreement, but it looked like she needed more convincing.

The plan was to pitch the tent on the common grazing – it was close enough to the house to keep his mum happy but far enough away from her watchful eye. They had a thermos flask for hot tea, and they would all bring snacks, DJ's mum would supply scones and cheese for their hungry stomachs. During the camping conversation with his mum, he'd neglected to mention they planned to camp down at Score Bay, close to Duntulm Castle. The journey would take at least an hour by bike – too far for him to get her permission so he decided not to tell her. What she didn't know wouldn't hurt. She would think they were on the hill or somewhere in Totescore. The boys didn't tell their folks what was planned either – just in case, they didn't want them to worry. Score Bay excited them the most because they would take a midnight walk to the castle and had talked about exploring the nearby Castledawn House which sat beneath the castle. Close to the shore the house had been empty for years and there was talk of it being haunted. This didn't put the three of them off – if anything, the idea of seeing a ghost made them more determined to go inside the once grand looking country house.

Blowing out the candle, DJ settled under the blankets. The thought of no school for two whole months made him happy. In the living room below, his mum pottered around, singing quietly. This made him feel even happier – she deserved to sing after the misery she'd gone through.

This summer was going to be totally bloody brilliant.

***

"DJ... DJ are you awake? DJ... We need water darling."

His mum's voice pulled him from a dream he now struggled to remember. With sticky eyes and hair all over the place, he jumped out of bed and dressed. First chore of the day was the water buckets. It was after nine, the grey sky above Linicro promised rain but he hoped it would clear up in the afternoon. He didn't mind the occasional shower creeping over from Waternish, but he hated when it poured all day and the Linicro rocks disappeared in the mist – on days like that his mum made him stay close to home. Filling the buckets, he remembered it was van day – Big Tam from Earlish and his mobile shop would pass and there was a chance his mum would buy him and Catriona sweeties – smiling he carried the full buckets back to the kitchen. His mum reminded him to wash his face and brush his teeth. He was hardly dirty – he did have morning breath, though.

From under the kitchen table, he grabbed a white enamel basin and half-filled it with scooped bucket water – a bar of Lifebuoy soap sat on a plastic tray nailed to the wall. Wetting his face with frigid water, he rubbed the sleep from his eyes – lathering his hands he scrubbed at his face and neck.

"Ears, don't forget behind your ears darling," said his mum.

"How can behind my ears get dirty?" he smiled.

This conversation they had had a million times.

"Ears," she said firmly.

Catriona sat on the living room floor, her blonde hair in pig tails, wearing a cute, chequered dress – she was in deep conversation with her teddy, totally oblivious to DJ and his ears.

Face washed and dried he took the basin of soapy water to the back door and threw it on the grass. One day they'd have a kitchen sink. One day. From his dad's shaving mug he picked up his toothbrush and a tube of Signal.

"A pea-sized drop please," said his mum.

"Stingy," he replied with a smile.

They had had this conversation a million times, too.

After a two-minute brush, timed by his mum, he rinsed his mouth with a glug of water and walked to the back door again – spitting the frothy mouthful on the grass.

His stomach gurgled, a sign he needed the loo. No running water meant no flushing toilet. The smaller of the two sheds had been painted primrose yellow by his mum, inside was a chemical loo. His mum bought this second-hand in Uig where it had been in a holiday caravan. The portable potty had a top tank filled with a smelly blue chemical and after finishing your business you pressed the flush button and the blue stuff poured in, carrying the waste to the bottom tank. On the hill, close to the house a septic tank was installed, everyday his mum emptied the waste into this concrete globe all but buried in the ground.

DJ kept a stash of comics in the loo to read whilst he sat on the plastic throne.

"Hands," said his mum when he reappeared in the kitchen.

"I just washed them," he replied.

"Hands," she repeated.

Another conversation they had had a million times.

After a breakfast of porridge and three slices of toast washed down with creamy milk from Norman's cow, DJ set about his second chore of the day – feeding the hens, collecting their eggs, and mucking out their house. Beneath the kitchen window sat a metal bin where the Layers Mash hen food was stored. He scooped the feed into a red bucket containing the remnants of porridge along with several eggshells – to this he added a half jug of water, using a wooden baking spoon to mix it into a thick, sticky mess. The stuff looked pretty gruesome and smelled funny, but the hens loved it. Bucket in hand and Catriona behind him he walked round the house shouting "Chook chook. Chook chook." Catriona, who loved feeding the hens, called them in her own way "Chookie chookie, chookie chookie." The birds gathered at their feet – ready for breakfast. DJ let Catriona spoon out chunks of the gritty paste and laughed as she tried to shake it off the spoon, on to the ground.

"Chookie chookie! Chookie chookie!" she shouted gleefully.

Once done he sent her back into the kitchen with the empty bucket. From the side of the henhouse, he grabbed the rust ridden shovel, went inside and scooped the hen poop into an equally rusty bucket, carrying and emptying it into the nearby compost pit his mum was cultivating for her planned vegetable garden. She'd marked out a patch of land behind the house. The ground was weedy and rocky, but Norman promised when his boy Derek was home from university, he'd get him to dig up the weeds, remove the rocks and prepare the ground for planting. Derek was studying in Glasgow, and when on holiday, he was a frequent visitor to the Shepherds Cottage. DJ thought he had a wee crush on his mum.

After poop scooping, he collected the eggs into a wicker basket belonging to the cottage's previous residents – his mum rescued it and cleaned it up. The egg haul was less than usual – meant he'd have to search the croft for hidden nests. DJ enjoyed mucking out the hen house and got satisfaction from seeing the poop covered floor clean. Twice a month he would wash down the cement floor with tobar water, scrubbing it with a thick-bristled byre brush, supplied by Norman – one of the many things he donated to make life easier on the croft.

DJ liked how Norman and Maggie helped his mum – it was like having your grandparents living next door. He'd no idea how old Norman was, but he looked ancient – maybe in his forties, balding with a big nose and friendly eyes, his face weather-beaten and his cheeks ruddy red. The man was strong, too – with massive hands, always covered in cuts and bruises and Band Aids. As well as working the croft he worked on the roads for the council. With his son and daughter at university he and Maggie had begun doing bed and breakfast during the summer. Maggie missed the children and liked to keep busy – always smiling and always wearing a sky blue, flowery pinney, her skin looked as weather worn as her husband's. She loved Catriona and loved looking after her, which suited DJ down to the ground as it meant he and the boys could go about their mischief making and not have to look after a four-year-old lassie. His mum says she doesn't know how they would've managed without the help of her neighbours – not just Norman and Maggie, but all the folk in Linicro had welcomed the family to the township. Norman and Maggie helped the most though and not a day would go by without one of them being in the cottage. Their croft was just the other side of the tobar, a big and friendly house with white-washed walls and a black slated roof. At the back were Norman's sheds and DJ liked to hang about there, watching him work on some piece of machinery – occasionally getting the chance to help.

Chapter 3

James and John showed up after lunch – just in time for big Tam's van. DJ's mum handed him a shopping list and money. It wasn't big list – she usually did the weekly shop in Portree after work.

The three of them pushed and shoved to get served first.

"Right, lads. Who's first?" said the big man with a grin.

DJ handed him the list whilst the brothers decided on what sweeties to buy. He loved the smell of big Tam's van. Sweet and inviting like their kitchen when his mum baked. It didn't take long for Tam to supply the sweeties and the shopping – with a cheerio and a see you next week, he took off down Linicro. Customers waiting to spend their money stood at the side of the road. The boys carried the shopping to the kitchen, dumping it on the floor.

"We're away up the hill," DJ shouted.

"OK darling, be careful and don't be late for dinner."

Each of them had a Crunchie and a bar of McGowan's chocolate covered toffee. They'd eat them on the common grazing where they would do a reccy for their first camping trip.

The hill behind the cottage was steep but not too steep, an easy walk for young legs.

At the top they climbed over the metal gate separating DJ's croft from the common grazing, rather than going through the fiddle of opening it.

DJ was last over and before jumping he looked back towards his house, and to the Minch and the hills of Harris in the distance – he loved this view and wished his dad was there to see it. The heather-covered ground was still moist, but firm under foot as they made their way to the large circular patch of grass slap bang in the shadow of the Linicro rocks. There they sat, not bothered about their bums getting wet and opened their Crunchies.

"It's perfect here for the tent," James said.

"Aye, nice and flat and soft," agreed John. "It'll be easy to pitch."

"Have either of you pitched a tent before?" asked DJ.

They looked at each other with raised eyebrows.

"Eh... No? Have you?" James asked.

"Nope. Should be fun though," replied DJ.

"When should we do it?" said John.

"What about tomorrow?" suggested his brother.

"Tomorrow's good for me. I have no plans," DJ laughed.

All three devoured their Crunchies and set about doing the same to their toffee bars.

***

In the evening at dinner, DJ told his mum about their camping plan.

"Remember you are looking after Catriona tomorrow. I'm at work," she said, handing him a bowl of boiled potatoes.

"Yep. No problem. We will go to the hill in the evening, after the boys have done the milking."

He scooped three potatoes and popped the smallest in his mouth, whole. When he first saw potatoes boiled in their skin, he wasn't keen to try. His mum told him the skin was the best part and it was good for you. He didn't believe her, but over the last year he'd gotten used to it and actually liked it – especially when the potatoes were lovingly coated with Maggie's homemade butter.

"Feed your sister, darling," said his mum.

Catriona sat in her wooden highchair, another gift from the previous residents. His mum had cleaned it up, sanded it down and painted it white. Feeding Catriona was a hit or miss affair – depending on her mood. Tonight, was a miss – she was too busy laughing to eat.

In bed, by the light of the candle he reread a Commando comic book. The story was set in Burma and the British soldiers had pitched a tent in the jungle hiding from the Japanese. He dreamt he was lost in the jungle and could hear his dad calling his name – no matter how hard he searched he couldn't find him. This was a recurring dream – although the location changed –it was always his dad calling out and DJ was never able to find him. Sometimes he woke up crying.

***

His mum woke him at six o'clock – she was leaving for her shift in Portree Hospital. In her white uniform DJ thought she looked like an angel – he never told her, but always thought it.

"Look after your sister and remember to eat," she said, kissing the top of his head.

His mum drove a ruby red Volkswagen Beetle which she absolutely adored – treating it as one of the family. DJ preferred his dad's Saab, but his mum hated it – she sold it not long after he died. She always looked happy driving her Beetle, and that made him happy.

Catriona woke up crying for her mum. DJ picked her up off the bed and shook her about – the tears turned to laughter. After feeding her Rice Krispies, he boiled the kettle and got a basin of soapy water ready. After washing Catriona, he got her dressed and she reminded him about her teeth.

"Teeth brush, give me teeth brush," she insisted.

He squeezed a spot of toothpaste onto her Snow-White toothbrush and did his best to brush her teeth – not easy as she laughed and wriggled about.

"Hairbrush, need my hairbrush," Catriona demanded playfully.

After a quick brushing of her blonde locks, she asked for pigtails. DJ had no clue and told her Maggie would do it. With her hand in his he walked the short distance to their neighbours. Maggie was in the kitchen as usual. Norman was in the byre. With a smile and wave, he left his wee sister to get her hair pigtailed. He'd chores to do, and more importantly – he had to ensure everything was ready for the camping trip. Tonight, was the night – he felt excited.

Chapter 4

The boys arrived at DJ's just after seven. On John's back was an ex-army rucksack with tent poles sticking out the top and, hanging from the bottom, a green ex-army sleeping bag. James carried the tent and a sleeping bag – Swiss roll like, tied with twine, hanging either side of his handlebars. They parked their bikes inside the front gate. It had rained in the afternoon, but a Minch wind had blown everything dry, and the sky was now a purple tinged blue – perfect camping weather. DJ's mum had packed cheese scones and sandwiches made with Maggie's homemade jam into a black and white Adidas shoulder bag. As a camping treat, she included three cans of Lilt and three Blue Riband chocolate biscuits.

"Remember boys. If you can't sleep, you can always come back here," she said, handing the bag to DJ.

"We'll be OK Mrs McKay. Don't know about DJ, though. Maybe he'll miss his teddy bear," James grinned.

They all laughed – except DJ, who made a face at James as if to say, I'm going to get you back.

"Where's your sleeping bag DJ?" John asked.

He'd forgotten it was in the storage room above – diving up the stairs he found the sleeping bag in a corner, covered in dust. Slapping off the stoor, he jumped back down the stairs. Three Cheerios later they made their way to the hill. On the common grazing they found their chosen camp spot, dumping the gear on the flat patch of green grass.

"Do you *actually* know how to pitch a tent, John?" asked DJ.

"Aye, don't worry. Duncan told me what to do. Easy, boy," smiled John. He emptied from his rucksack the tent poles, metal pegs, a flat-headed hammer and a plastic groundsheet. Untying the twine, he rolled the tent on the grass, ready for pitching. Next, he barked orders and DJ, and James followed his every word. The groundsheet was first, then the tent poles were pushed through metal ringed holes in the canvas until the tent stood erect. The bottom corners were pulled tight and metal pegs pushed through the metal rings and bashed into the soft ground with the hammer. John hammered the front and back pegs firmly into the ground. Once the middle pegs were in place, he secured the rain sheet over the top like a professional – job done. They hoped it wouldn't rain but better to be safe than sorry. Walking around the construction, John checked the tension of each corner and once satisfied gave the thumbs up to DJ and James. The tent had seen better days and smelled a bit funny, but it had no holes and although only a two-man affair, it was plenty big enough for the three of them. Inside they spread their sleeping bags and stored their supplies – it was after nine when they finished, but it wasn't dark. The sun had sunk in the west leaving the sky a pyjama pink, purple. The distant hills of Harris and the further Uists silhouetted on the horizon like a serrated knife blade.

Sitting on the grass they divvied up DJ's mum's scones along with the Lilt.

"When we go to Score, I'll bring firelighters, we can collect driftwood from the shore and have ourselves a wee campfire," said John.

"Brilliant," replied DJ, who wished they could have a campfire now. Next time they'd be more prepared.

After scoffing the food, they took a wander to the drystone walled sheep-shearing fank. A summer night breeze blew up from the shore, but it wasn't cold. Wearing his Golas, DJ had to be careful traversing the boggy patch between themselves and the fank. The brothers wore black ex-army boots bought from the same shop as the tent, but it was James who put a foot wrong and sunk up to his knee in dark, peaty mud. DJ and John howled with laughter as they helped free James from the foot-sucking mud. Lucky it was just one leg – it wouldn't take long to dry. Scaling the stone wall, DJ wondered about the folk who constructed such a sturdy boulder barrier. The Linicro fank was pretty massive – a stone square beneath the rocks of Linicro. Dotting the green grass inside, were huge boulders that had probably rolled down from the hill long before the fank was built. The biggest was Transit van size, and that's where they headed – climbing it they pushed and pulled each other, laughing and shouting. Their voices echoed off the Linicro rocks and bounced around the hill. Stars appeared above them – winking and welcoming – scattered across the night sky. In Edinburgh, you rarely saw many stars – but in Linicro – especially on crispy clear winter nights – millions upon millions of them stretched across the North End and beyond. DJ loved it and wished his dad, who knew all about stars and astronomy stuff could star gaze with him.

Bored with the rock, they headed to the sheep pens and dipper. DJ had yet to see this in use as dipping season was in the spring when he was at school. One day, though. One day he would ask his mum to let him skip school – just for a day. The dipper was a creepy looking bath filled with soupy thick grey water – a stinky, chemical smell hung in the air, as the boys took turns jumping across it. Not that it was difficult, the dipper was a wee bit wider than a normal bathtub – a lot deeper though – with pens either side of it. Sheep would run into the murky water and crofters pushed them under using a wooden contraption that looked like a brush with no bristles – once suitably soaked, the sheep were herded into the opposite pen. DJ was desperate to see it.

Finished with the dipper, they sat where the township sheared the sheep. Backs against the boulder wall, DJ looked forward to the upcoming sheep shearing fank – it would be good smelly fun. They strolled to the far end of the fank, looking over to the deserted village of Greulin. The ruins of the thatched black houses were excellent places to explore. It was creepy, though, especially at night. Locals said ghosts of old women and children could be seen walking the fields of Greulin – best to explore there during the light of day.

By eleven o'clock they were back at the tent and sipping hot sweet tea from a tartan Thermos flask. Between sips they talked about the trip to Score Bay and about the girls they fancied. The girl conversation continued inside the tent, wrapped in their sleeping bags – fully clothed. DJ was stuck in the middle, and it was him who talked the most about the lassies. Well, one lassie in particular. Claire Ross from Uig – she was in the same class as him and he'd a real fancy for her. With long black curly hair, freckles on her nose and blue, blue eyes she was something and she played for the school's netball team. At last year's school Christmas dance DJ found out that Claire liked him – her pal Annie McKinnon from Staffin told him. He was happy about it but unsure about what to do. Dancing the Grand Old Duke of York dance with Claire, she kissed him, and it was the best thing ever. John was the only one who had had a real girlfriend, a lassie, in the year below him. DJ and James called him a baby-snatcher, but secretly they were jealous.

"Ask her out, man. You will be a second year soon and it's embarrassing you have never had a girlfriend," laughed John.

"Aye, maybe," DJ replied.

They talked into the night eventually surrendering to tired eyes. DJ went to sleep thinking about Claire and that Christmas dance kiss. What a girl. What a kiss.

Chapter 5

DJ woke up dying for a pee. John was already up and out. James snored under his sleeping bag.

"Morning, boy," said John.

"Pee." DJ ran behind the tent.

"What time is it?" he asked.

"Around seven."

A low hanging mist waited to be burned away by the morning sun. The dew damp ground released a perfume of grass and cow pats.

"Wake up my brother, will you? We need to pack up and get home for the milking."

With James awake they dismantled the tent, rolled and tied it up. After checking for rubbish, they made their way down the hill towards DJ's.

"So, when are we going to go to Score?" asked James.

"We will need to plan it well boys. My mum would go off her head if she knew we were so far away," said DJ.

"You are right. She would be worried about you missing your teddy bear and goodnight kiss," laughed John.

"I will bring my teddy and you can kiss my bum," said DJ.

"Aye right," John smiled.

"Here's what I think. If we are going to Score, we should spend two nights there. Make it worth the journey. We can tell our folks we are camping in the fank for one night and at the top of peat road by the burn the following night," said James.

"Good plan," said his brother.

DJ nodded in agreement, climbing the gate to his croft.

After arranging a meet up at the quarry, the brothers jumped on their bikes for home. DJ dumped his sleeping bag upstairs and changed his t-shirt.

"DJ is that you? Water please," shouted his mum.

Catriona was awake and in her highchair, his mum sat at the living room table reading The Weekly News.

"Well... How was it? Did you miss me? Did you miss your sister?" his mum smiled.

"Miss me. Miss Mummy?" repeated Catriona.

He didn't answer – just smiled as he grabbed the buckets in the kitchen.

Norman came by in the afternoon. DJ was on the lawn, sweating and struggling with the push-pull mower. Bess was asleep at the front door, legs twitching and tail wagging – dreaming about chasing rabbits, no doubt.

"You're doing a grand job there, laddie. I hear you were camping on the hill last night. How was it? See any ghosts?"

"Really good. No ghosts. Next time we are staying out for two nights."

"Two nights? You're hardy right enough, boy. Here, take this milk for your mum. Tell her Maggie will be round later. I think she's making fairy cakes."

He handed DJ two bottles of milk – real old-fashioned type bottles, very thick glass which had been reused hundreds of times – no tin foil lid just a greaseproof paper circle secured with an elastic band.

"See you, boy." With a smile and wave Norman was gone. DJ put the milk in the fridge and Catriona joined him out front.

"Maggie's making fairy cakes for you," he told her.

"Cake from a fairy?" she asked.

"Aye. With white icing."

She beamed and ran back inside to tell her mum the exciting news. Bess remained oblivious of the cake news, DJ continued mowing, the day was hot, the sky was blue and cloudless. With each push and pull he thought about Maggie's cakes – she was a brilliant baker and he looked forward to eating more than a few of them.

After dinner and after a game of hide and seek with Catriona and Bess, DJ took off for the quarry.

"Back by ten darling," said his mum.

Behind the hen house was a makeshift bike shelter – constructed by his mum. Four wooden legs and two sheets of corrugated plastic for a roof – it wasn't ideal, it only sheltered the bikes from vertical falling rain, a rare occurrence in windy Linicro. When he got his new bike, he would make space in the back shed to ensure it was safe from the elements. His old bike was a Christmas present from his Grandparents in Fort William – a gold-coloured Raleigh Jeep which he loved but it was now getting small for him, and he'd big plans to spend the money he'd been saving on something very special.

Miss Murchison was standing at her doorway, watching life go by – she smiled and waved at DJ to stop.

"How are you DJ? How's your mammy? How's Catriona?".

The caileach lived alone with her Cairn Terrier Kenny and was always looking for somebody to chat with.

"Aye, they're fine Miss Murchison. How are you? Will you be needing any work done?"

"You could come by and cut some firewood and kindling. There'll be a pound in it for you," she smiled.

"Sure. No problem. How about the day after tomorrow? I could come by after doing my chores. Probably one o'clock. Would that be OK?"

"That would be fine, son, that would be just grand. Here, have one of these." From her cardigan pocket she produced a packet of Pan Drop mints. He took one, saying thanks, and continued up the road to the quarry.

"We'll see you the day after tomorrow then," she shouted. DJ waved – another pound towards his bike fund put a smile on his face that lasted all the way to the quarry.

James and John were waiting on him. He parked the bike against the fence and climbed the rusty red gate. The boys sat on the grass beneath the waterfall. It was a warm night and there wasn't much of a breeze – DJ hoped the midges wouldn't come out and ruin his fun time.

"Did you tell your folks about the camping trip?"

"Aye. My father said it was fine, but we have to behave ourselves," James grinned.

"Behave ourselves. That's a good one," DJ laughed.

"We will need to be organised this time. OK?" said John.

"Sure. I'm always organised," said his brother.

John slapped him across the head. Playful – not hard.

The hot weather had reduced the quarry's stream to a trickle, the green moss that coated the waterfall was bone dry and brittle. DJ picked at the grass, throwing the green blades at James as they discussed the Score Bay trip. They'd need enough food and drink for two days. Firelighters, matches, pen knife and oilskin raincoats. John delegated responsibilities. DJ would bring his dad's pen knife – his mum had given it to him – but she worried it was dangerous and that somehow, he might chop a finger off. He knew where it was kept and could easily nab it without getting caught. They'd have to bring their wellies too – night-time adventures required keeping their feet dry. The more they talked, the more excited they got.

Did I ever tell you this place is haunted DJ?' asked John.

"What the quarry? Aye right. Sure it is."

"I'm serious. Ask any of the old folk, they will tell you."

"Haunted by who?"

"Not who. What." James said.

"Aye right," DJ replied.

"No word of a lie," said John.

"Well... Are you going to tell me?"

"OK... The old folk say there are nights when a mist rolls down from the hill into the heart of the quarry."

"And?"

"In the mist there is a beast."

"Rubbish, don't believe you," said DJ.

"It's the truth boy. Why would I lie? They say the beast hides in the deepest part of the quarry. Some folks say they've seen it."

"What does it look like?"

"They call it yellow paws in English, but its Gaelic name is Spogan Buidhe."

Yellow paws didn't sound scary, but Spogan Buidhe was pretty creepy.

"Be careful DJ. Especially when you are walking or cycling on a misty night. Spogan Buidhe might get you," laughed James.

"Aye right."

"I'm telling you it's true boy," smiled John.

"What? Have you seen it?" DJ asked.

"Not seen, but I heard it," replied John still smiling.

"Heard what… Liar," sneered DJ.

"Seriously. One night I heard something. Like a low growl. Thought I saw a shadow in the mist. Scared the heck out of me."

DJ looked closely at his pal's face but couldn't tell if he was joking – he hoped he was.

Before ten, they walked and talked down the road – pushing their bikes. It was decided the following weekend they would head to Score. John impressed upon the younger boys the importance of sticking to the same story when talking about the trip to their parents – they didn't want to arouse suspicion. At the top of their road, the brothers said cheerio, jumped on their bikes and zoomed downhill towards home – DJ continued to walk. Spogan Buidhe was on his mind, and he checked the hill for mist – none, but he jumped on his bike and cycled home like a madman.

Reading his Sparky comic by candlelight, thoughts of Spogan Buidhe were still with him – he was sure the boys had made the story up, but it scared him a wee bit.

He went over what he would say to his mum about the camping trip – he didn't like lying to her, but telling her they would camp in the fank wasn't such a big lie, was it? They were only going to Duntulm – it really wasn't a big deal, less than an hour away. Downstairs the phone rang – it made him jump. Probably his Granny from Edinburgh, she phoned nearly every night. When they first arrived, the cottage didn't have a telephone line – the phone box outside Linicro Post Office was their only connection to the mainland, but after meeting Maggie and Norman, they offered the use of their phone, anytime, day or night – they meant it too. That's how kind they were. After six months, the Post Office Telecommunications Company installed a big white phone in the living room. This made life easier for his mum – especially when she began looking for work – on the wall above the phone was a list of emergency numbers for DJ – top of the list was Norman and Maggie.

He dreamt he was in the quarry; a soupy fog surrounded him. There was a growl, weird sounding, like a cassette tape playing at slow speed – an echo too, definitely not a dog. He tried to run, but as was often the case in his dreams he found he couldn't. He tried to fly – sometimes in dreams he could – but his feet were stuck in boggy ground, and he was sinking. The growl got louder, closer. From deep in the quarry's heart, he saw two yellow eyes – looked like something from a Scooby Doo cartoon – but scary. His heart pounded; his feet stuck. The yellow eyes moved closer, became bigger – growling echoed all around. Totally frozen and terrified, tears fell – he knew he was going to die, just knew it. There was a hand on his shoulder, it wasn't Spogan Buidhe – it was his dad. Smiling. Telling him it was OK, no need to be scared. Funny, his dad didn't open his mouth when he spoke – DJ heard his voice in his head. Soft words of comfort, he felt safe, the fear of yellow paws evaporated. Holding his dad's hand, his feet were free of the bog.

He woke up crying.

Chapter 6

It was mid-morning. DJ was sat outside the house taking what he thought a well-earned rest after completing his mandatory chores. As well as his usual jobs his mum had asked him to give the back shed a good tidy. He wasn't happy about it but did as he was told. Now he could relax. With his mum at work and Catriona next door with Maggie he had the rest of the day to himself and planned on doing very little. He had a couple of Commando comic books to read and with the sun moving higher in the sky, the front of the house was the perfect reading spot. From his vantage point he saw James and John's father's blue Marina van take off from their house. Not long after he saw the black shapes of the boys on their bikes. Five minutes later they were at his gate. All smiles.

"Alright boys? Didn't expect to see you today. Thought your father had you working on the croft?"

"Aye. We were meant to be fixing the fence at the back of the house, but my uncle Alistair is sick, so our folks are off to Staffin to visit with him. My mother's cooked him some grub," said John.

"Oh... Right...Well, I hope he'll be fine. So, what's the plan? Mum's at work and Catriona's with Maggie so I'm free as a birdy."

"Aye you look like a bird right enough. A wee sparrow," James grinned.

"Aye and you look like a big fat hen... Laying eggs... Chook chook," DJ retorted.

"Thought since we have the afternoon off, we'd take you on a wee trip. Somewhere you've never been before," smiled John.

"Oh aye. Where?"

"Surprise... Get your bike."

"I'll need to pop into Maggie's. Tell her I'm off out."

"No problem boy. We'll be passing her house anyway."

A quick hello and goodbye to Maggie and the three of them set off down Linicro, turning off at the cattle pens on the mud track to the fank.

"The fank? Not much of surprise," said DJ parking his bike against the pen's concrete wall.

"Just wait boy," smiled John.

Bypassing the dry-stone wall structure, they headed towards Greulin. DJ had been through the deserted township many times but didn't mind visiting again. Talk about a perfect day. T-shirt wearing weather, hot with heather-infused hill wind keeping foreheads cool.

"Not like I've never been to Greulin before boys. Is this the surprise?"

"It's not," said John.

"Hope you're ready to climb the hill," James said.

"Aye. I'm always ready," smiled DJ.

Greulin fascinated DJ. The hamlet had long been deserted and he'd try to picture what it was like when it was full of families and life. Black houses with thatched roofs. Crofters and their wives, tending to their beasts. Children running around, laughing and playing. He wondered what had happened to the population and why it was deserted. If ever there was a place for a beautiful wee village it surely was here under the watchful eye of the Linicro hills. Their journey continued high on the hill that looked over Greulin. It was pretty steep, but the ground was firm and the heather sparse. As they climbed higher the wind got stronger. A welcome relief as they were all totally sweating. Eventually they reached a plateau. DJ had never been this side of the hill before, way opposite the Linicro rocks. What a view of Kilmuir you got. Endless and all the way down to the Camus Mor. The Minch rippled under the summer sun, blue and beautiful and the Harris hills looked like you could touch them, they appeared that close.

DJ was dying of thirst.

"Boys. I'm so thirsty. I'm desert dry,"

"Told you we should have brought some juice or something," said James to his brother.

"There's a stream up here, runs down the side of the rocks. You can slurp from that," John replied.

"From a stream? What if there's sheep poop or cow dung in it?"

"Don't worry boy. It runs fast. Clean and clear enough for your delicate body," smiled John.

Sure enough, a stream appeared as they neared a rocky escarpment. DJ scanned the area for a good spot to take a drink. John crouched down in front of him and began slurping from the stream that ran over well washed pebbles.

"Here DJ, it's cold and clean," John said, wiping water from his chin.

James joined DJ and they drank down as much of the cold stuff as their bellies allowed. Tasted just as good as tobar water. Maybe even better.

Hydrated they continued on their journey over terrain that DJ noticed getting rockier and rockier. They finally reached a stretch of flat, heather-covered hill.

"You going to tell me where the heck we're going?" pleaded DJ.

"Nearly there boy. We're nearly there."

Five more minutes of walking and they were at the edge of a high cliff. DJ couldn't believe his eyes. At the base of the cliff was a big black loch. He'd never seen anything like it.

"Wow. A loch. How come you never took me here before?" he asked.

"Just came to mind as my folks left for Staffin. Not been here in a while. Think it was three years ago when I was with my father gathering sheep for shearing," said John.

"Man, it's totally beautiful and so secluded. Can we swim in it? Has it got a name?"

"Loch Sneosdal. I wouldn't swim in it. They say it's pretty deep. God knows what lies beneath," smiled John.

"Can we go down? I want to walk around it."

"DJ, give us a minute to catch our breath will you. It's just a loch," James said.

They sat as close to the cliff edge as they dared, resting up and getting their second wind. DJ took it all in. This was an amazing place with an amazing view.

Breath caught; John led them across the cliff ridge until they came to a grassy hill running down the far side. They cut down at speed making their way to the loch edge. The view across the water to the high cliff was breath-taking. DJ thought they could be on another planet it was so wild, rocky and remote. The peat dark water shivered in the breeze. Who knows how deep it was? DJ was a good swimmer, but he wasn't brave enough to attempt a dip in Sneosdal's icy water.

"My father said they used collect diatomite from here," said John.

"Diato... What?"

"Diatomite. It's a rock or something. Was a thriving business he said. Years ago, I think."

"How would they get it to the road? Don't fancy carrying a load of rocks all the way to Kilmuir," said DJ.

"Probably a horse and cart. Many folk used to keep Clydesdale horses. Huge beasts. Strong and hard working. Maybe they used them here."

With pebbles in their hands each of them tried to throw the furthest. John's aim was true, and his pebbles hit the middle with a distant splosh. Wasn't long before they had to start the long trek home. They didn't retrace their steps. Opting to walk at the base of the hill all the way back to Greulin. Not as easy as it looked. The hill was pock marked with rabbit holes and fallen rocks. The ground was hard on the ankles. DJ was absolutely starving by the time they made it back to the Linicro pens and their bikes. He didn't have the energy to cycle home and told the boys to go on without him, he'd see them later. Pushing his bike through the front gate he saw his mum was home and his dinner was almost ready. Beef stew with mashed potatoes and onions. At the table he wolfed it down like someone who'd not eaten in days. His mum was happy to see him eat so well. Catriona ate a wee bit of the mashed potato but didn't touch the meat. DJ scoffed her stew portion too.

Chapter 7

Next morning DJ woke with stiff legs and muscle pains. Both legs felt the way they did after running cross country in PE class. After breakfast and his chores his muscles had loosened – the pain was all but gone when he headed towards Miss Murchison's – her front door was open, he gave it a knock.

"Hi Miss Murchison, its DJ."

"Come in, son. Come away in," she replied.

She was poking at the fire, putting a square of peat on the red and orange flames – it wasn't even cold outside, he supposed it was because she was old and felt the cold easier.

"You said you needed wood cut Miss Murchison?"

"Eh?" she said, her hand to her ear.

She was a wee bit deaf and didn't like wearing a hearing aid – complaining that it whistled too loudly.

"You have wood needing cut?" he half shouted.

"Oh, aye, that I do. The wood by the shed. I'll be needing it cut so they will fit in here," she said pointing at the fire.

"I'll be needing kindling too DJ."

She placed the poker in its holder, satisfied the peat would burn.

"Come on laddie, I'll show you. So how are you? How's Catriona and your mammy?"

"Aye fine. Everyone's fine."

"That's good. That's good. And your tearaway pals. What nonsense have you been getting up to then?"

"Oh, nothing much. The usual. Went through Greulin yesterday on the way to Loch Sneosdal. My first time there. Bit of a trek but it was worth it."

"Loch Sneosdal you say. That's a fair hike laddie. You must've been tired when you got back."

"Aye. A wee bit. Legs were a bit stiff this morning".

"Do you good. The walk. Fresh air. Do you good. Greulin you say. Don't know if I told you this but my folks were from Greulin. Well, they lived there as children."

"Really?"

"Oh, aye son. Oh aye. It was a thriving place at one time. Long before my time mind you,"

"Bet it was beautiful then. Why did people abandon it? Such a perfect place to live. I mean with the hills and all."

You're right there laddie. You're right there. Folk moved on. The crofts were wee you see. Not big enough to make any kind of living. With mouths to feed many of the menfolk moved away from the area altogether. My mother's family moved to Earlish. My father's moved here. They met at dance in Uig. He was a fisherman. His boat was berthed at Uig pier. Mother would tell me stories of ceilidhs and dancing. Sounded grand to me when I was young."

"I bet," smiled DJ.

A pile of pinewood, sat by the shed, it had been sawn into rough planks, the bark still attached. At the side of the shed was a wooden trestle, DJ dragged it round and

Miss Murchison produced a bright red Bushman saw and a small axe – both looked brand new.

"These should do the trick. Bought them in Portree last week." Miss Murchison handed DJ the tools.

"Aye, these will do fine. I'd better get on with it," replied DJ.

"Let me know if you need anything. Cold drink, a sandwich – anything you want, son. Just ask."

"Thanks. I will."

The old girl toddled back to the house leaving DJ staring at the wood pile. Looked like more than an afternoon's work to him, and he was sure there would be more than pound in it. The money didn't matter so much. Miss Murchison was old and needed his help but anything she paid him, brought his dream bike ever closer. Bushman at the ready he picked up a plank, placed it in the trestles' groove and began to saw – it took a while to find a rhythm. The wood oozed sticky stuff and smelled the same as the air freshener tree thing hanging from the Beetle's rear-view mirror.

After an hour of sweat-producing work Miss Murchison brought him a Tupperware jug of cold water and a mug of sweet tea along with two mint Yoyo's – cutting wood was thirsty business and the chocolate snack was welcome anytime. It took four hours to cut and stack the wood behind the shed where her coal and peat sat. He set about chopping the kindling – his hands sticky and aching – it took a good half hour cutting the wood into thin strips. Lucky the axe was super sharp. He placed a bunch of kindling in a bucket, took it inside, by the fireplace – they would be tinder dry and ready to use the next day.

"Och you're a good boy, so you are. What would I do without you?"

"No problem, anytime. I'd better be making a move. Mum will be making the dinner. If you need anything else done just let me know."

"The grass around the house will be needing a cut. Do you know how to use a mower?" she asked.

"We have an old push-pull mower Norman gave us. I know how to use that."

The old girl laughed as if he'd just told the world's funniest joke.

"Och that's too old-fashioned. I have a petrol Flymo, brand new, mind you. Too heavy for me, but I think you could manage it as long as you're careful and don't run over your toes," she said with a grin.

"I'll be careful. Don't worry."

A Flymo – wow! He would look forward to that.

"Aye well, here's your money," she said, pulling a wee tartan purse from her cardigan.

Expecting a pound note, his eyes widened when she produced a fiver.

"You did a grand job DJ. You deserve more than a pound."

"Are you sure Miss Murchison?"

"Oh Aye. Don't be daft, son. Take it."

He took the note, thanked her again, and told her he'd be back in a few days to cut the grass. Walking home, he was happy as anything – a fiver was a lot of money. They could use some of it to buy supplies for the camping trip – the rest would go to his bike fund.

His dinner was just about ready when he arrived.

"Hands DJ - and wash your sister's too," his mum said.

At dinner the courage needed to ask permission for two nights camping evaded him, but he was determined to ask before bedtime. After reading Catriona the three pigs' story for about the thousandth time – he decided it was now or never.

"So… At the weekend we thought we would camp for two nights. Is that OK?" he asked gingerly.

"Where?" said his mum, flicking through The Oban Times.

"First the fank then up the peat road to spend a night by the burn."

"You sure you can stay away from me for that long?" she smiled – a good sign.

"Yes mum… I'll manage."

"OK darling. As long as you promise to behave."

Wow! She didn't even put up a fight or anything.

All she asked was he finish his chores before leaving – that was it!

***

The days passed with DJ doing his chores, playing with his sister and reading comics. It had rained heavily and he didn't see the boys but tomorrow they would cycle to Uig to buy supplies from the baker's shop. In bed, he made a mental list of what they needed. His mum would prepare scones and cheese – the boys would bring sandwiches with salmon spread. Having a campfire, meant they could heat up tinned food – maybe soup, baked beans, and definitely a couple of tins of Irish Stew.

It was early afternoon when James and John arrived at DJ's. The rain had stopped, leaving the road wet and shiny.

"Hope it's dry at the weekend," DJ said as he jumped on his Jeep.

"Forecast said it would be windy but dry," said John.

"You listen to the weather forecasts? Are you bodach* now?" DJ smiled.

"The radio's always on in the house. Radio Scotland. Can't help but hear the weather."

"Don't suppose they have the shipping forecast on Radio One," laughed DJ as they took off up the road.

At the quarry, James shouted, "DJ... Watch out for Spogan Buidhe. He's coming to bite your bum."

"Aye right," said DJ.

They puffed their way up the Totescore hill – the road levelled out at the top but was pretty bumpy. It didn't stop them from racing each other – speeding towards Uig. Being the biggest and the strongest, John always won. The summer months brought many tourists and their cars to the island and the North End was a popular destination – the boys had to be careful on the single-track road. Most of the time the tourists slowed for them, letting them whizz by safely.

From the top of Uig it was all downhill. Freewheeling round the hairpin bend, they zoomed – ignoring man and beast until the road dipped at the River Rha Bridge. The wee hill slowed their approach to the dual carriageway where Uig Police Station sat close to the fork in the road. At the bakers they propped their bikes at the side of the shop. With their pooled cash they bought

---

* An old man.

cans of coke, Mars bars, a bottle of Robinsons diluting orange, two tins of baked beans, two tins of beans with the wee sausages and three tins of Irish stew. Also purchased was a big box of Bluebell matches, Eveready batteries for their torches and a box of firelighters. They each bought an ice lolly and leaving the shopping bags with their bikes they crossed the road and sat on the wall of the River Conon Bridge. James had a Raspberry Splice, John a Top Ten and DJ, his favourite – Tiger Mint. Below them the peaty water of the Conon rushed towards Uig bay.

They divvied up the supplies – each carrying one plastic bag, swinging from their handlebars. They pedalled as far as the Rha Bridge, then got off the bikes and walked uphill towards the hairpin bend – they were in no hurry to get home.

"I was thinking, Friday night would be good to explore the castle, leave Castledawn till Saturday afternoon," said DJ.

"Scared of the ghosts, are you?" James smirked.

"It's not that, if we go during the day, we'll be able to see more. Maybe find something valuable, treasure or something." After a moment's thought he added, "What if there's a safe?"

"You're dreaming DJ," James replied.

"The bank who own it stripped it long ago. Inside's a mess – I've looked in the windows and the place is totally empty,' said John.

DJ was frightened to go at night – during the day was less scary, definitely – so he kept up his argument.

"You never know. They might have missed something."

"Let's see when we get there DJ.".

"Agreed," said James.

They walked round the hairpin bend and once at the bealach road they got back on their bikes. From the top of Totescore they sped towards DJ's – the faster the better. The camping supplies were stored in the back shed – hidden from Catriona's wee hands. Being an hour before dinner, they crossed over to the smiddy.

"Oh, man. I forgot to buy batteries for the radio. Next time remind me," DJ said, play punching James.

"You told your mum about camping at the fank and at the burn?" John asked.

"Our father said we don't need to do the milking, means we can leave in the afternoon," James added.

"Mum's fine about it. I will tell her we are taking the bikes to the fank track and leaving them at the cow pens. Easy," DJ smiled.

"Aye, good idea," James said.

"My ideas are always good."

"Aye right," said John sarcastically.

To keep his mum happy, DJ did the washing up after dinner. Catriona wanted to help, he lifted her on to a wee stool and let her wash the knives and forks in the basin – he dried.

The following day he was back at Miss Murchison's, as promised, totally excited about using her Flymo. Norman had one, but it was massive – far too heavy for DJ's skinny arms. He'd watched him swing that beast about many a time and was confident he could use the old woman's new mower. She was at her front door when he arrived.

"Hi Miss Murchison. I've come to cut your grass."

"Eh?" she said.

"Your grass. I've come to cut your grass!" shouted DJ.

"Oh... Right you are son. Come with me."

In the corner of her shed was a green and white Flymo – not as big as Norman's and as she said before it was brand spanking new.

"Do you know how to use it DJ?" she asked.

"Aye. I've seen Norman use his. It's not difficult."

"Well, it's got petrol in it already. Give the place a good short back and sides eh," she laughed.

"No bother, Miss Murchison."

"Oh... And DJ... Watch your toes. Don't want to be calling an ambulance."

Laughing to herself she left DJ to get on with it. Following exactly what he saw Norman do he put his shoulder under the mower handle, using the lower handle to carry it flush to his body. It was heavier than it looked, but he managed, just. Miss Murchison wanted all the grass around the house done. Flipping the mower switch, he pulled hard on the cord and the engine roared to life. Flymos hover on a cushion of air and DJ began swinging it from side to side. It wasn't as easy as Norman made it look, but he soon got the hang of it, the long grass behind the house had no chance. It took two hours to finish but the time flew past and by the end he was swinging the mower like a professional. As well as watching out for his toes, he had to watch out for pebbles hidden in the grass, they could damage the blade or get spun out from underneath faster than a speeding bullet. Norman had warned him of this, saying they could do some damage if they hit someone or something.

Once finished, he surveyed the area with pride – freshly cut grass and petrol fumes, the smell of summer – made him feel good inside. Before storing the mower in the shed, he brushed away the moist grass from the underside, as per Norman's instructions – making sure he cleaned in-between the blade. Wiping the underside down with a rag he carried it back to the shed. Job well done.

Miss Murchison came out of the house to look at his handiwork.

"Another grand job you have done DJ. A grand job indeed."

From her purse she produced another five-pound note. Pocketing the money with a big grin, and even bigger thank you, he waved her goodbye. Tired but happy he walked home – totally excited about the next day's camping trip.

He really couldn't wait.

Chapter 8

DJ's excitement level was off the charts – he counted down the hours whilst doing his chores, wishing time would move faster than the snail's pace it took to get the morning finished. His mum had a doctor's appointment in Uig, and he was in charge of Catriona – at least it took his mind off the time. It was four o'clock when the boys arrived at the gate. John's bike had a homemade trailer attached, loaded with stuff and secured with a thick elastic rope with hooks.

"Where did you find that?" DJ said, staring at the contraption.

"Made it. Pretty good, eh?" replied John.

DJ admired the ingenuity of it – it looked like a trailer you would see hitched to a tractor, only smaller. A square wooden box with high sides, John had used a metal arm and plate bolted to the back wheel and attached it to a hitch on the trailer – simple and strong looking.

"Made it from a pallet we had in the tractor shed and that old pram we had in the byre, remember last year we were going to make a go-kart with the wheels? Still could I suppose."

"It's bloody genius. Cycling up the Hungladder road will be easy without bags hanging from the handlebars," said James.

John unhooked the elastic rope and added DJ's sleeping bag and his food filled Adidas bag. He secured it all by pulling the rope tight as anything and hooking it underneath the trailer. DJ's mum appeared at the door; her eyes fixated on the trailer.

"It's just two nights boys. Not an expedition to the North Pole," she smiled.

"Just a wee bit of fun, Mrs McKay," James said.

The three of them took off down the Linicro road.

"Be good boys and be careful. No mischief."

They pedalled passed the track leading to the fank – hoping nobody would notice where they were heading. There was no hurry. At Kilmuir Post Office they made a pit stop, buying three Cornettos to cool them down and to give them a sugar boost before ascending the hill at Hungladder. Cresting the top, DJ was sweating and out of puff, as was James but John was not even breathing hard. After clanking across the metal cattle grid, it was all downhill to their destination. The weather had stayed true to Radio Scotland's report. No rain, but there was a cooling wind coming off the sea as the boys freewheeled through Score Bay.

The spot chosen to pitch the tent was not far from the road – a flat circle of grass close to the shore. With a stream nearby, it was pretty perfect. Below, the rocky shoreline curved past Castledawn House, along to the Duntulm Castle cliff. They set about making camp and once the tent was pitched, John chose a spot for the campfire, instructing DJ and James to find medium-sized boulders to form a stone circle. Score Bay was all rocks, so it was an easy task.

"Firewood boys. We need firewood and we need to hurry. The tide is coming in," said John.

Scrambling to the shore they realised they need not worry about the tide – the place was awash with wood to burn, and it did not take long to collect a healthy supply of driftwood to feed the fire. John produced a shiny steel axe from his backpack and started to cut up kindling. With fire lighters it was easy to get the campfire going. They sat round it – looking into the sparking red flames – although there was a salt breeze, it wasn't cold.

"Who's hungry?" John asked.

The biking had left them starving. Luckily, John was organized, He'd not only brought a tin opener and a pot – he'd brought paper plates, cups and plastic spoons too.

"Found the plates and spoons in our pantry. Think they were used for my sister's birthday party last year," he said.

DJ opened his Tupperware container full of cheese scones. James pulled out the Thermos flask filled with cold water and got the bottle of diluting orange ready for mixing.

"What do you fancy? Beans and sausages or Irish stew?"

They agreed on beans and sausage – John opened the tins and poured them into the pot, placing it on the fire and giving it the occasional stir with DJ's dad's pen knife until the beans bubbled and popped.

"We only have enough cold water for one night," said James.

'You hear that?' asked his brother.

"What?"

"The stream you cretin! You know – the stream with water."

"What? For drinking? God knows what could be lying in it up on the hill. Could be a dead ewe or something," said DJ.

"Don't worry. After we eat, I will boil the water in the pot. Easy, boy."

He'd thought of everything, and they were soon tucking into food– washed down with cold Robinsons Orange Barley Water, sipped from paper cups.

"No rubbish boys. Black bag everything. Don't want anyone complaining we left trash around for their sheep to eat," said John.

With the rubbish in the bag, John placed a rock on top so it wouldn't blow away when the wind gusted off the Minch. The fire burned red, and orange and the sun sank, leaving behind a strip of sky the same colour as their fire. It wasn't dark. During the summer, it never got dark, not really. Unlike the winter when the long nights were pitch black.

The sky turned a darker shade of blue, streaked with pink.

"Castle, boys," said John, pointing across the fields.

Castledawn House sat between them and Duntulm Castle – right on the shore, almost. A thin strip of salt-stained grass separated it from the rocky beach. If ever a building looked out of place on Skye, it was that big house with its red sandstone bricks, wind worn and ominous. To DJ it looked like the houses he'd seen in Edinburgh's Grange – Castledawn wouldn't look strange there, but it definitely looked weird here. The building looked creepier now than it did when they first arrived.

With no shining sun Castledawn looked less benign in the Duntulm gloam. Tomorrow they'd have a look inside, not tonight, *definitely*.

The rocks and jagged cliffs of Score are monumental, DJ never tired of seeing them. Hard and aged they sat grey in the night light – grey turning to black. The road was quiet this time of night with the waves crashing on to the shore providing the perfect soundtrack for a night-time adventure. Time and weather had taken its toll on the once grand looking Duntulm Castle. DJ had seen a painting of it in a book his mum had, and it looked pretty cool when it was the clan home to the MacLeods and MacDonalds – now it was roofless and at risk of collapse. Still, you couldn't help being impressed as it sat in rugged majesty on top of a steep sea cliff.

Crossing the fence, they walked towards the ruins. The summer night sky was now a deep purple – it was still far from dark. DJ could see the shape of the Harris hills across the Minch – silhouettes undulating in the distance. The winking eye of the Stornoway lighthouse informing them they were not alone, and everything was just fine. Climbing over the crumbling stone wall, they entered the body of the building. A solitary window looked out to sea and the nearby Duntulm Island. Beneath the sill, a steep drop to the rocks and the cold waves below. DJ, like most North End children, had heard the story of the nanny who let the baby fall from this very window. Dashed on the rocks. Her punishment? They put her in a small, oar-less boat and pushed her out to sea, never to be seen again. She and the baby's ghost are meant to haunt the Castle. Locals would tell stories of seeing apparitions and hearing the cries of a baby. DJ didn't know if it was a true, but it was a good story, if a wee bit creepy.

"Let's go to the dungeon," smiled James.

The large hole underneath the side of the castle was where they headed – they sat inside for ages, talking and laughing. DJ didn't think it was a dungeon – John insisted it was where the clans kept their prisoners, feeding them salt meat and not giving water so they'd die of thirst. He pointed to the scratches on one of the walls, saying thirsty prisoners used sheep bones as a means to escape. DJ found it hard to believe, but John was convincing. He said that on particularly still nights you could hear bone scrape against stone – ghosts trying to escape.

On the grass beside the dungeon, they sat, looking down towards the shore – their eyes focused on Castledawn. Talk about scary! DJ was glad, they were at the castle and not there at the house.

"Tomorrow, boys. We will get inside, and I don't want you crying like babies if we see a ghost," John said with a big grin.

"How will we get in?" asked DJ.

"There are broken windows at the front. Should be easy to climb in."

"What if someone catches us?" said James.

"Who is going to catch us? The owner? His ghost? Nobody cares about the place. It belongs to a bank in Edinburgh. What? You scared the bank manager might catch us?" laughed John.

"Just worried. Don't want our father to give us what for," James said.

DJ would've loved to get what for from his dad. He would've loved for his dad to be annoyed at him for getting caught trespassing – he wished his dad was alive.

"Let's go. See if the fire's still going. I've got some chocolate biscuits," said John.

The thought of a sweet treat got them on their feet, and back to the tent. All the way back DJ couldn't keep his eyes off Castledawn, from different angles the building appeared to change shape – probably just a trick of the light.

Feeding the fire with more driftwood, and with smoke and sparks climbing above their heads, they sat eating Blue Riband biscuits and talking about girls and music and cars. DJ liked any excuse to talk about Claire Ross and to think about her. Did that mean he loved her? He didn't know, but he knew he liked her. A lot.

John doused the last of the fire's glowing embers with water from the stream. DJ and James would never think of doing such a thing. They crawled into the tent and their sleeping bags – DJ felt toasty, his eyelids were heavy – he drifted off to the sound of waves crashing and to thoughts of Claire Ross and Castledawn.

Chapter 9

They woke to the sound of rain bouncing off the tent. John peeked outside and saw a thick haar had blanketed Score. Visibility was zero, but he knew the sun would eventually breakthrough and evaporate it. After eating a breakfast of salmon spread sandwiches, they ventured out. The sea mist had all but disappeared, although the far hills of Harris remained invisible, cloaked in grey. The rain had stopped, and John set about making a fire.

"What would you idiots do without me," he said, pulling driftwood from under a plastic sheet.

"What do you mean?" asked DJ.

"Do you think you can light wet wood? I covered the wood pile last night. Knew it would be showery in the morning. I listen to the weather forecast."

"Maybe you could get a job as a weatherman," smiled his brother.

"You're boring enough," DJ laughed.

Drinking barley water, they sat watching the tide go out and the Harris hills appearing in the distance.

By mid-day the sun was high, and the Score was transformed from a damp grey colour to sea blue. Puffy white clouds floated across the Minch towards them and soon everywhere was summer dry. A sea breeze rolled up from the shore, salt and seaweed tinged. Two seagulls screeched and squawked at each other as they perched on a nearby 'Passing Place' sign.

"We need more wood for tonight boys," said John.

Walking the shoreline, they were soon on the rocks in front of Castledawn. DJ thought it looked sad rather than scary in the sunshine and, in its day, it would've been a beautiful family home. John pointed to the vestibule and a glass-less window, saying if they were to go inside, there would be the point of entry. DJ was excited and a wee bit apprehensive about breaking in. But, first things first, firewood – the tide always supplied enough driftwood, along with a weird array of rubbish.

"What would you do if we found a dead body," DJ asked.

"What do you mean? On the shore?" said John.

"Aye. Maybe a sailor or a fisherman who fell overboard and was like, drowned or something; covered in seaweed and half eaten. What would you do?"

"Run a mile," smiled James.

"Aye me too," DJ agreed.

With arms full they headed back to camp. The fire had gone out, John would set a new one when they got back from Castledawn. For a while they sat on the wee stone bridge that crossed their water-supplying stream. A few locals drove past, smiling and waving. A bodach rumbled by on a red Massey Ferguson 135 tractor and a big smile on his face – a roll up cigarette stuck to the corner of his mouth. He waved; the boys waved back. Tourist cars stopped near the Castle, others carried on towards Flodigarry or Staffin. Funny how a simple thing like watching traffic could be fun – especially when you could see fancy foreign cars and dream of owning one yourself.

Back at the tent they prepared for their Castledawn adventure.

With torches in hand and penknife in pocket they set off across the field singing Rod Stewart's Tonight's the Night – before long they stood in front of the dilapidated house.

"Must have cost a fortune to build this place. My father told me they brought all the sandstone from Edinburgh. The owner wanted an Edinburgh styled house on Skye," John said.

"I've seen houses like this in Morningside and the Grange. Big fancy places," said DJ as he peered through a grimy window – from what he could see the room was stripped and empty.

A glass vestibule enclosed the front door. Looked like it had been added a while after the house was built. The once white paint that covered the wooden frame had turned a sickly grey. The wood looked rotten and some of it had given in to time and salt.

"Check this out. We climb through here and hope the inside door is open. If not, we will need to find another way," said John.

Most of the vestibule windows were cracked or broken and covered in green slimy stuff. At one side some of the glass and wood had given up the ghost leaving a large hole and climbing through was a piece of cake. At the front door, John reached to turn the brass knob. It clicked and he gave it a push – it didn't move, but he was sure it was open. He gave it a harder push and felt resistance. The wood had probably warped with age and needed a wee bit more force.

"Mon boys, help me give this a good push."

With all hands on the door, after the count of three, they pushed hard – the door scraped open, ever so slightly. Something was jamming it at the bottom. They gave it another push; it opened a wee bit more. One more big push opened it halfway, and one by one they slipped through the gap. John saw the parquet floor tiles had lifted and wedged under the door, no wonder it was stuck.

They stood in the hall – it wasn't dark, but it was pretty gloomy and empty. There were a couple of rooms either side of the hall and a wooden staircase sat right at the end. Light filtered through holes in the ceiling, the place reeked of damp and stoor coated the floor. The walls were stain-streaked, years of leaking rainwater had left its mark. DJ stuck close to his pals.

"Where first?" said James.

"DJ's choice," replied John.

"Any door is fine by me," said DJ, nervously.

They moved towards the door on the left – heavy and wooden – John twisted the doorknob and pushed it open. Peeking in they saw it was empty of furniture, only a huge marble fireplace and mantelpiece remained. Looking above them DJ saw that the ceiling was covered in black mould and water stains – he could make out the fancy cornicing and the centre rose was tar black. Torches on, their bars of light illuminated the shimmering dust hanging in the air. The room wasn't dark, but they had brought the torches and they wanted to use them.

Suddenly there was a loud creak above them and DJ's heart jumped in his mouth.

"What was that?" he said, shining the torch up into the ceiling's corners.

"Relax, probably the wind. Old houses make noises," said John.

They walked around the room, shining the torches on floor and walls. The floorboards creaked under their weight – puffs of dust blew up with each step they made.

"Big living room, eh?" James said.

"Aye big living room with nothing interesting in it. Come on, let's see if there's anything worth looking at in the other rooms," John replied.

Last to leave, DJ heard something whisper quietly.

"Did you hear that?"

"Hear what?" asked James.

"Don't know. Like a wind or... I don't know, something."

He was shy to say it sounded like a voice.

"Probably a draught... or a ghost," John added in a scary voice.

"Aye, probably," DJ replied with a shrug.

Each ground floor room was the same: empty and stripped of anything of value – totally lifeless. At the back of the house was a big kitchen with a huge soot black cast iron range. The boys' mother used an Aga in their house, but it was tiny in comparison. Other than a woodworm infested table, there was nothing of interest whatsoever. In the far corner was an archway – they walked through, finding a set of narrow steps corkscrew twisting to the bowels of the building. It was dark, and the smell was bad. Three torch beams lit the way as they descended the stairs. The lower they got the stronger the smell was – a foosty smell mixed with something else, sickly sweet, rotten. DJ and James stopped midway and let John carry on to the bottom. There was a door, boarded with planks of thick wood – a faded sign, nailed to the middle plank, read 'Danger. Cellar. Keep Out'. The floor was sludgy and sticky – a black mould bog.

"Boys, check this out!" shouted John.

Hesitantly, DJ and James joined him on the viscous, stinking bottom landing.

"Wonder what's in there?" James said.

"Not sure I want to know," winced DJ.

"Man, it really stinks down here," said James covering his face.

John tugged on the middle plank, it was stuck fast – each end, hammered deep with big iron nails.

"We need a crowbar to get these off," he said.

"We could bring one next time," replied James.

"And some gas masks," DJ added.

"Yes, it's rotten down here. Worse than up top," said James.

"Aye, maybe a drain's burst in the cellar," John offered.

Turning, they walked back up to the kitchen.

"This place is boring. There's absolutely nothing here," said DJ with a disappointed look.

"Come on, let's check upstairs. You never know, could be a box of treasure waiting," smiled John.

"Aye right," replied DJ, doubting there was anything of value in the old house.

Climbing the wooden staircase, light creeped through a dirty window at the top of the stairs, a wind too. James peeped out of a cracked, slimy green glass pane. He could just about see the Castle. A long corridor mirrored the ground floor. Light rays from ceiling holes indicated that the roof was probably open to the elements. The walls were dirty and slimy wet, the damp floorboards had given way to rot, and exposed joists were woodworm riddled. John turned on his torch, shining it along the corridor's length.

"Watch your feet here," he warned.

There was a toilet – a broken commode – lying on the crumbling floor. Again, they checked every room – the back bedrooms and the front. Nothing – each room, stripped and smelling awful – worse than what came from DJ's septic tank. Black mould spread across the ceilings and ran like tears down the walls. It was hard to imagine anyone living here and DJ wondered why the house had been left to wrack and ruin. The room by the stairs was the master bedroom. It had a large marble fireplace and a window that looked out to the Minch. In the corner an open door led to a bathroom with an old ceramic tub smeared in black and brown gunk. Above the bath, a small window filtered yellow light. The smell was overpowering – they didn't hang around.

"Boring boys, let's get out of here. No treasure for us," said a smiling John.

"Hold on... Look," DJ pointed to the wall opposite the bathtub.

"What now, DJ?" sighed James.

"Look at the wall, the tongue and groove. There's a door there. I'm sure of it."

John stepped into the bathroom and looked closely at the wall – there was slither of space between the wood panelling which his big fingers tried to push, then pull.

"DJ's right. It's a door. My fingers are too big. DJ, see if you can open it with your girly hands."

Smirking, DJ tried but couldn't get leverage to pull. He ran his hand up and down the wood, feeling for a secret lock. On TV shows hidden doors always had secret locks – here though, there was nothing.

"Leave it DJ. Next time we'll pop it open with a crowbar, no problem at all," said John.

They headed back down the stairs – DJ was happy to be getting out of the place.

"We will come back with a crowbar, see if there is anything hidden in the bathroom and the cellar," said John.

DJ would be happy never to look in the cellar – that place gave him the creeps.

Nearing the front door DJ heard something – a whisper, definitely, coming from the front room. Oblivious, the brothers headed to the vestibule. DJ stopped; he heard the sound again – this time louder. Entering the living room, again, a voice, church mouse quiet, seemed to be coming from the fireplace. It didn't sound scary – if anything, it sounded familiar.

"DJ, what you are doing. Come on, man. I'm hungry!" James shouted.

"Aye OK. I'm coming," he shouted back.

"DJ."

He recognized the voice.

"DJ."

It was his dad – no doubt about it, but how? He walked to the fireplace and stood still, listening. Nothing, maybe it was wind coming down the chimney. Something moved – his heart pumped faster. What the heck? He crouched and looked up the lum – a soot covered pigeon flew out and at him. His hands raised to his face, the bird flew over his head, flapping – losing balance, he fell on his backside. The bird was on the floor, wings stretched as if it was trying to take off. It looked at DJ, DJ stared back – the bird ignored him and began preening itself, flapping intermittently to get rid of the stoor. DJ exhaled, smiled, and picked himself up. He shouted on James, but he and John had already climbed through the window and stood outside.

"A pigeon came down the chimney!" shouted DJ.

"Leave it," said James.

"It will get out the same way it came in. Just like us," John smiled.

"But what if it gets stuck?"

"Chase it into the corridor and shut the door. It will find its way out this window."

"OK... Give me a minute. Let me chase it out."

The pigeon was now perched on the mantelpiece, still cleaning itself. The soot made it look like a wee crow. He walked towards it, slowly – thinking he could catch and let it out the window. The pigeon was too busy with its preening to notice him creeping towards it. Edging closer – arms out-stretched and eyes closed, he pounced. The bird took off, fluttering above him, it flew out the door. He smiled – nearly got it... nearly. Something on the mantelpiece caught his eye. Between the marble and the wall, he could see the corner of a piece of paper sticking out – it looked like an envelope. With thumb and forefinger, he prised it from its hiding place. The once white paper was now stained brown. Could be a treasure map, you never know. There was writing on the front – black ink, faded. Two words, handwritten. 'Forgive me.' Strange. He lifted the flap – inside, a letter.

"DJ your pigeon pal flew out. Hurry up. She's looking for you. She misses you," James laughed through the vestibule window.

"She says she loves you. Come on boy. Time to go," called John.

Folding the envelope, he shoved it in his pocket – to be read later. Maybe he would keep it till he got back home, not show the boys – if there was anything about treasure or a hidden safe, he would tell them. It would be a good excuse for another camping trip.

Chapter 10

Around the campfire they sat scoffing Irish stew. The sun was creeping over the Minch and with barely a breeze blowing, it was positively warm – perfect midge weather.

"Bit of a let-down, Castledawn, absolutely nothing in the place," said James with a mouthful of stew.

"Told you, the Edinburgh bank stripped it after the war," replied John.

"Wonder if there is anything in the cellar? Must be something there. Why would they board it up?"

"So wee gnaffs like you and DJ wouldn't fall and break your necks. The floor probably collapsed. That's the reason for the danger sign."

"Aye, but if they wanted to hide something a sign like that up would keep folk away. We should definitely go back. DJ, what do you think?" asked James.

He didn't want to think about what could be lurking in the cellar.

"Might be something behind the door in the bathroom."

"Aye, maybe," agreed John.

"Bet that's where they hid the gold bars," James laughed.

"Dream on," his brother replied.

"You never know."

"He's right. You never know. That room could be the one place that was not stripped. Maybe nobody knows it is there," said DJ.

"Aye, well, next time we can check out," said John.

"What if that is where the hellish smell is coming from?" speculated James wiping his nose with the back of his hand.

"Could be where the bodies are hidden," suggested his brother.

"What? Do you think there is someone dead behind the door?"

"Not someone, DJ... Something," grinned John.

"Don't worry. If there is a body, it can't hurt you. I'll protect you," said James putting his arm round DJ.

"Get off!" DJ shrugged his arm away.

"Anyway, next time we will be more prepared," said John.

"Aye, boys, bathroom and cellar next time," replied his brother.

"A cellar is a good place to hide a safe."

"You're dreaming DJ. If there was a safe the bank would've emptied, it. Bet they lost a bundle of money on that place."

"Aye... Maybe. But do you think they know about the hidden room? *We* nearly missed it."

"That is the question boy. That is the question."

"Next time we will find the answer," said James.

"Wonder why nobody bought the house from the bank? I mean it's fancy and big, right next to the sea... Right next to a flipping Castle. How come some rich English guy never bought it?" DJ asked.

"Told you. It's haunted," said John." Nobody wants to live there."

"What ghosts? Did you see something?" asked his brother.

"I heard something... In the living room. Weird, like someone whispering," said DJ who felt stupid to say it sounded like his dad, so he said nothing more.

"That's the midges out," said John getting to his feet and changing the subject. "Finish eating and we will go for a wander, these blighters will eat us alive."

Walking on the road towards the Castle, the air was thick with midges – biting every part of their exposed bodies. They quickened their step.

"Where are we going?" asked DJ.

"Wherever there are no midges," laughed James.

Near the Coast Guard's house, John cut off-road, heading towards the lochan in the field below the house – DJ and James followed behind, half running. By the black-watered pool there were fewer midges, and the surface of the lochan rippled by the faintest of breezes wafting over from Kilmaluag. Circling the water they threw rocks into the peaty depths – seeing whose stone made the loudest plop. DJ wondered if any fish lived in the lochan's deep, dark water.

The Kilmaluag wind picked up and took them back to the campsite. After a snack of treacle scones and cheese they zipped themselves into the tent – hoping the midges wouldn't reappear and bite them in their sleep.

DJ stood in front of Castledawn. The house looked different –like someone was living there. Summer flowers grew in window boxes on ledges and smoke rose from the chimney. "DJ," his dad's voice, no longer a whisper.

He was at the front door, his hand outstretched, turning the shiny brass doorknob – the black door clicked open, he stepped into the hall. A coat-stand with jackets and hats and a big mirror stood on the floor. Turning to look outside he wondered what happened to the vestibule where they had climbed in earlier. When he turned back, he was standing in the hall of his flat in Bruntsfield. His dad was calling from the kitchen.

"DJ, DJ, I'm here son."

The hall expanded, the closer he got to the kitchen, the further away it was, his dad's voice, fading.

"DJ. In the kitchen son. I'm here."

He tried to run, the kitchen was no closer, it was like he was jogging on the spot. The voice stopped – he was standing outside the master bedroom upstairs in Castledawn. A shiny brass handle turned, and DJ slid inside. A large bed, fresh linen and by the window, a writing table and chair. A roaring fire burned in the marble fireplace. The bathroom door creaked open, the splashing of water. Fear balled in his ribcage as he moved towards the bathroom, he'd lost control of his legs, they belonged to someone else, not him. Through the doorway, inside was bright and clean, too bright – blinding white. The enamel bath was spotless, like glowing. Water dripped from a brass tap, overly loud. In the water-filled tub, a young boy with coal black hair, his skin, ghost white; his clothes, muddy and torn. DJ's heart raced, he was petrified; he couldn't steal his eyes away – an overwhelming feeling; he had to keep looking. The sound of his heart and the drip of the tap vibrated in his head. It was impossible not to look at the boy – like when you see a road accident. The black-haired boy seemed like he was sleeping beneath the water. DJ leaned closer, not by choice. The boy's eyes opened, mile wide and white, porcelain like, doll's eyes, missing the pupils. DJ screamed, no sound. The boy's hand grabbed DJ's wrist, wet, cold.

His eyes opened, he was in the tent with his sleeping pals either side of him, he breathed a sigh of relief – it was only a dream. DJ wondered what time it was – early morning, definitely. They would head home today after breakfast. Listening to his pals breathing he thought about the boy in his dream, he was small, young maybe around six or seven. The dream was so vivid, Castledawn was so real, it scared him a wee bit. What about the letter he found? Why would someone write Forgive Me on it? Why not a name or an address? It was all a bit weird.

After a breakfast of salmon spread sandwiches, they packed the gear on to the trailer, James bagged the last of the trash. The morning sun was warm, a firm breeze rolled off the bay as they pushed the bikes up the Score Road – it was far too steep to be bothered cycling. Anyway, there was no rush to get home. DJ loved Score, the cliffs and the falling rocks gave the place another worldly feel, like they were on another planet or something. He recalled the first time his mum took him and Catriona to Duntulm Castle, he was in total awe. He felt something, like he knew it or had been there before, an attraction pulled him towards the cliffs, castle, and bay. No words could describe the feelings he had, there was just something about Score that made him feel... Something.

Peaking the road at Hungladder, they crossed the cattle grid and jumped on the bikes, bombing it down the hill. Biking through Kilmuir was easy enough, they had the wind at their back. Arriving at DJ's they unloaded his gear and arranged to meet in the smiddy the following afternoon. DJ dumped his stuff upstairs and changed into fresh clothes.

"DJ is that you?" shouted his mum.

"DJ zat yoo," Catriona copied.

"We need water son."

"Water bucket son," laughed Catriona.

Leaping down the stairs, he breezed into the kitchen with a smile. Catriona was on the floor, playing with two headless dolls, DJ wondered if the dog had chewed off the other doll's head or had Catriona removed it so both dolls were the same?

"The wanderer returns," said his mum.

"Aye. That's me," smiled DJ, grabbing the water buckets.

"What? No kiss?"

With a sigh louder than was needed, he kissed her cheek.

"Missed you darling. Did you have fun? Did you behave?"

"Yes, and yes," he replied with a slight hint of Castledawn guilt.

As tobar water filled the buckets, he thought about his dream. The sound of his dad's voice, clear in his head. The cold wet touch of the black-haired boy on his wrist. Talk about strange – in the tent he had checked his wrist, more than once, to make sure it was dry.

After dinner DJ and his mum sat on the sleeper seat out front, while Catriona played with her dolls on the lawn. Bess snoozed beside her.

"So tell me?" said his mum.

"Tell you what?"

"DJ, I love you, but you are not a good liar. Where did you boys camp?"

How the heck did she know?

"What do you mean? We camped at the fank, then up by the burn."

"DJ... I know you didn't. So tell me."

"How do you know?"

"We walked to the Post Office the other night, your bikes weren't at the pens, and I doubt you cycled across the bogs to the fank."

Mums always know.

More lies would be pointless – he told her the truth.

"Och... Mum... I didn't want to worry you. We went to Score bay. Camping at the shore. You know how much I like it down there."

"DJ it's awfully far. What if something happened? An accident or an emergency?"

"The Coastguard's house is close. We would go there. The boys know Mr Mackenzie. Nothing to worry about mum."

"I don't like it when you lie to me. Look... If you want to go again, there's a phone box near Mr Mackenzie's. You have to call. OK?'

"OK. No problem," he smiled, surprised that she was taking his deception so well.

With her arm round him his mum dragged him in for another kiss. He struggled; she pecked his cheek.

"So what did you get up to then?" she asked, freeing him from her embrace.

He told her everything. Well, everything apart from breaking into Castledawn – even though it was not really breaking in. He left that out – just in case.

Before getting into bed, he pulled out the Castledawn envelope. The candle flickered as he lifted the flap and pulled out the note. The paper had turned yellow, and like the writing on the envelope the ink had faded, but it was easy enough to read:

'I beg for forgiveness.

I have committed the unforgivable, there is no one to blame but me.

Those poor boys.

I did it for my wife, she was so sick, they said it was the only way to cure her.

They lied.

The guilt I carry is too much.

Only God can judge me now.

Cornelius Black

Castledawn

1855.'

Disappointed he folded the note and placed it back in the envelope – he'd hoped for a map, maybe even the combination number of a safe, something valuable at least – all he got was some guy saying he was sorry for something.

Castledawn was alive, each room, warm and friendly. Someone whispered "DJ". A young voice. Drawn to the back stairs, like a moth to a candle, DJ was unable to stop. Bedroom – open, a fire, burning, wood crackling within the flames. Gliding forward as if skating on ice, powerless to resist – he was inside the bathroom. The black-haired boy was waiting in the tub, under water. His eyes opened, gruesome cueballs, wider than wide, his hand reached for DJ's wrist.

He woke up, heart pounding, a knot of fear in his stomach his eyes staring at the ceiling. The black-haired boy's wet grip was cold, deathly cold.

Chapter 11

The sound of voices downstairs woke DJ. Maggie talking to his mum. He'd fallen into a deep dreamless sleep after his nightmare. Getting dressed he thought it weird that he'd had the same dream two nights in a row, weird and scary.

He dived down the stairs.

"Morning lazy bones," said Maggie.

"You must have been tired darling. Look at the time," said his mum.

It was eleven o'clock. He'd never slept that late. Never.

After a quick bowl of lumpy porridge, he left the ladies talking and went about his chores. It was another fine day, and he was looking forward to seeing the boys later – excited to tell them about the letter. Mucking out the henhouse was first; he shovelled the hen poop into his mum's compost heap and washed down the floor with a bucket of tobar water. When they first moved in, he found a shepherd's walking stick in the shed. A long grey stick topped with a sheep horn. This he grabbed and walked up behind the house to the big fern patch. Some of the hens had taken to laying there and he was hopeful of finding egg treasure. Prodding and swiping the undergrowth, he was careful not to inadvertently stand on a laying clucker. One of the broody hens jumped out of the ferns, cluck, cluck, clucking away –

a hidden nest sign. Crouching in the green, spreading the ferns he hit the Jackpot – a nest with six eggs. Lifting his t-shirt to create an egg hammock, he gently cradled them to the kitchen.

The last of the morning jobs was refilling the water buckets. At the tobar he stooped to scoop the water. A dark shadow rippled in the flowing stream – white eyes opened wide, staring at him. The boy from his dreams, black hair water wavy. DJ stumbled back in fright, dropping the bucket and getting his trainers wet. Heart, beating ten to the dozen, fear burning in his chest – he looked back into the water, his reflection rippled before him. What the heck? Was he seeing things? Hallucinating? Maybe he was still tired from the camping trip? Rescuing the bucket, he filled both to the brim, carrying them back to the kitchen a wee bit quicker than usual.

Maggie heard about the Score trip.

"Your mum tells me you've been naughty," she smiled.

"Yeah. Should've told her. Had fun, though."

"I'm sure you did. I know what you three rascals are like. Did you see any ghosts in the castle?"

"Nope. They must have been out," he said, grinning.

"Did you go to Castledawn House?"

"Eh... No... Passed it when we were gathering firewood from the shore."

"Nothing spooky there?"

"Nope. Nothing. What... Is it haunted?"

"So they say."

"Do you know anything about the place? Its history. The people who lived there?"

"Oh, aye. A wee bit. Ask Norman. He knows more than me."

"Aye, I will. It must have been a nice house in its day."

"Look at it now. Left to the wind and rain," said Maggie.

***

After dinner he crossed over to the smiddy. John and James were on their way.

"DJ."

His dad's voice.

"DJ."

A whisper repeated.

He stopped in his tracks – there was no-one around. He looked up towards Miss Murchison's – the old girl was walking her dog. Something moved in his peripheral vision. His eyes turned to the smiddy – standing at the door, behind the thistles, his dad, a big smile on his face. DJ blinked and his dad was gone.

No way!

He spun around, checking the front of the house, spun back, checking the smiddy.

Nobody.

A car horn beeped, and he almost jumped out of his Golas. A long French Citroen had come down the road and braked in front of him. The lady driver gave him a friendly smile. Heart pumping, he smiled back, and waved as if to say sorry. The car carried on down the road – in the backseat, four kids looked out the back window, smiling and waving like mad. DJ gave them a big mad wave back. At the smiddy door he checked for footprints, a sign of disturbance – but there was nothing. Wishful thinking, wishing his dad was here, a bit creepy too. Climbing the fence, he sat outside waiting for the boys. He didn't fancy sitting in the smiddy alone. His mind was playing too many tricks. That's what he thought, anyway.

Gazing out to the sea, DJ thought about the last time he saw his dad. A normal day. A school day. Both sat eating breakfast in the kitchen. His dad reading the Scotsman, occasionally glancing over the broadsheet and winking at him.

"See you tonight, boy. Be good," his dad's last words.

DJ didn't even reply, just smiled as his dad touched his cheek, another wink and he left for work. That was it. The last time he saw his dad alive. Since then he has tried desperately to remember what they had talked about the night before; he couldn't remember, and it made him sad. Most of the time he tried not to think about it, but sometimes, sometimes, all he could do was think about it.

"What's up with you?"

John's voice startled him.

"Nothing. Been waiting for you two."

"I brought batteries. Time for some music," said James.

"And I brought these," John held up three Crunchies.

"Nice. Something I want to show you. Let me get it from my room," said DJ.

"What? Your teddy bear," James smiled.

"Aye, right."

The brothers climbed into the smiddy, DJ hopped the fence, to fetch the letter. A minute later he was climbing through window. John and James were singing along to

Angelo by Brotherhood of Man. DJ joined in – singing the chorus at the top of their voices, so loud the whole of Linicro could hear.

"Boys, I found something in Castledawn."

"Found what? And is it valuable," grinned James.

"This," he pulled out the envelope.

"Wow! DJ found a piece of paper. Better call the Free Press. This is front-page stuff," laughed John.

"Ha Ha. Very funny. It's a letter, but it is strange. Listen to this."

He read it to them.

"What do you think?"

"Doesn't make any sense," said James.

"What do you think DJ?" John asked.

"Sounds like he did something bad.'

"Aye, but what?"

"He did something bad to some boys?" suggested DJ.

"Sounds like he did something bad and killed himself. That's a suicide note DJ," said John.

"You think so?"

"Aye, man. If it's real... Could be somebody wrote it as a joke,"

"What? Someone wrote a suicide letter for a laugh. What's funny about that?" said James.

"Just saying. Might be one of the locals. God knows how long it's been lying there.'

"Maggie says Norman knows stuff about Castledawn. Next time I see him I'm going to ask," said DJ.

"I'll ask my father. See if he knows anything. Sometimes the old folk know things, but they never want to tell you. Like it's some big secret or something."

"And there's something else," DJ said sheepishly.

He told them about his dreams. 10cc's Dreadlock Holiday played in the background. He didn't tell them about the whispering voice of his dad, he wasn't even sure if it was a whisper or just a voice in his head. He wasn't ready to tell them about seeing his dad or the reflection of the black-haired boy in the tobar water, not yet anyway – they'd think he'd gone bonkers.

"I've said it before, and I'll say it again DJ. You're weird," grinned James.

"Don't you think it's funny, having the same dream two nights in a row?"

"Doubt it means anything, though," said John.

"Anyway, forget about your weirdness. We're thinking about a trip to the Rha tomorrow. You interested?" James asked.

"The Rha? You know I'm interested. You need me to rescue you if you fall in and get your feet wet," smiled DJ.

"Aye, right," said James.

"We'll cycle along the bealach, dump the bikes and head down to the river. I know where a cracking waterfall is with a deep pool. If it's hot we can have a dip," said John.

They hung around the smiddy for another hour. Talking and listening to Radio 1.

***

DJ played with Catriona and her dolls. His mum sat at the table drinking coffee and reading the West Highland Free Press.

"Mum, do you believe in ghosts?"

"Sure I do. I saw one."

"Really? Where?"

"In your great granny's house. I was probably about your age."

"Seriously?"

"I'm serious. It wasn't long after she passed away and I think it was her."

"So? What happened?"

"She lived in South Queensferry. Her house was old, Victorian. Beautiful place with views across the Forth. When she died, me and your granny spent a couple of weeks there tidying it up. She had to sort out her mum's legal stuff. We slept in her room, both of us in her bed. One night I woke up needing a pee and I saw a woman in white, sitting at the vanity table looking in the mirror and brushing her hair. I was so scared I hid under the blankets for ages. I would've stayed hidden till morning if I hadn't been bursting for the loo. When I was brave enough to look, she was gone."

"So you think it was your granny?"

"I believe it was."

"What about here. Do you think this place has ghosts?"

"If there are I haven't seen them. Why?"

"Just wondering."

In bed after reading the Hotspur DJ pulled out the Castledawn letter – reading and rereading it. Was it a suicide note? He thought about letting his mum read it but knew there'd be questions to answer about where and how he found it. He couldn't wait to see Norman to get information about the folk who lived there before and to ask if the place really was haunted.

Castledawn. This was no dream – it felt real. Slipping through the hall, the living room had a roaring fire, there was a sofa and chairs and he wanted to go inside but his feet wouldn't allow it. Gliding up the stairs, he was floating. Fear in his chest, his heartbeat, loud, echoing through the house. Powerless, the forward motion continued, inevitably drawn to the master bedroom. The bed, unmade, the fire burning bright, orange and red – the colour of the room. A magnetic pull to the door in the corner. Fear level high, his breathing – quick and shallow. The bathroom door, opened, a loud creak, too loud. His tiptoes dragged, caressing the floorboards. Running water and a loud splosh, like someone dropping a boulder into a lochan. Bright room, ultra-white, glowing. A gurgling noise from the tub. With all his strength, he resisted, no use – his body floated forward. Peering over the edge of the bath, he saw the black-haired boy, skin pale white, almost see-through. Without wanting to, DJ leaned in. His hands on the edge of the tub, trying to stop his forward motion – he couldn't. Heart pounding in his chest and ears – he knew what was coming. Cueball eyes, wide. The black-haired boys head rose above the surface, his mouth opened like he was going to speak – no sound. He stared at DJ, thick black water and bits of bracken gurgled out of his mouth, down his chin and chest. The bath water turned oily black. His wet hand grabbed DJ's wrist tight. DJ heart stopped; he woke up.

Breathing fast and full of fear, he scrambled to light a candle – the striking match illuminated a shadow on the sloping ceiling. Boy sized. It disappeared.

He sat out of bed, feet on the floor, trying to work out what was happening. His wrist was wet. Wet and cold. What the heck?

Chapter 12

DJ woke with gummy eyes; he watched a moth bounce about on the tongue and groove ceiling. The room was oven hot. He checked his wrist, dry with no marks. Sitting up, he saw his candle had completely burned down – a circle of wax and a wee black spot was all that remained. He'd forgotten to blow it out. Getting out of bed, he opened the skylight window as wide as it would go. A warm breeze blew in, if *his* room was boiling, he reckoned the day would be roasting.

At breakfast his mum asked why he was so quiet. He said no reason, but there was. His mind tried to process his nightmare, the wet wrist and the shadow on the wall. Did it happen or was it still the dream? It must've only been in the dream – nothing else made sense.

He told his mum he was off to spend the afternoon on the banks of the Rha. She told him to be careful. She worried too much – what's the worst that could happen at the river? He'd fall in. He was a good swimmer, so no danger there. He waited at the Totescore road sign; the boys were halfway up the road.

"Alright?" he smiled.

"Boy it's hot today. A wee swim will be nice," said James.

"Och, the water's too cold for DJ's city skin," laughed John.

"Aye right," DJ replied.

It was far too warm to puff and pedal up the hill so they walked to the top of Totescore. The Linicro sky was blue and cloudless, and the Minch was green and still. Reaching the top, they jumped on their bikes and raced towards the bealach road. They cycled the road to Staffin until John announced they'd arrived. Dumping their bikes on the grass, they headed downhill. John knew the perfect spot for swimming. From the road the Rha was hidden, it's only seen when you legged it down and you come to a deep rocky ravine. The whoosh of flowing water was music to the boys' ears. DJ had been to the waterfall near the Rha's bridge in Uig – it was easy to find because it had a path, but he'd never been this far upstream. Descending the bowl-shaped ravine, DJ saw an impressive-looking waterfall gush into a dark pool – peat stained with a bitumen black middle. At the water's edge, they gazed at the waterfall – DJ loved it. This secret place was their own, nobody could see them, and the bowl shape was a total heat trap. With no hint of wind, the air was moist; a mossy damp smell permeated every nook and cranny. Sun rays filtered green light, tropical jungle-like... without the snakes.

"Wow. It's magic here," exclaimed DJ with an excited smile.

"This is where the touries don't come. Bet you there's trout here," said John.

"Is it deep? Looks it," wondered DJ.

"Don't know. Pretty deep, I think. Maybe six feet,"

"Nice."

DJ picked up a pebble, lobbing it into the pool's murky middle. It made a satisfying plonk as it disappeared into the depths, leaving an ever-increasing circle rippling towards where they stood. Hot and sweaty from biking, the still air offering little relief, John was first to strip to his underpants, walk into the pool and launch his body like a torpedo, under the peaty surface. Popping up with a gasp, he sprayed water from his mouth with a big smile. His feet just about touching the bottom as he stood in the middle of the pool, water just beneath his chin.

"Come on, you two. The water's lovely. It's *not* deep," he shouted, his voice echoing around the ravine.

James and DJ quickly stripped. James charged in like a mad man towards his brother – shouting and laughing. DJ was more cautious – not because of the depth, he was a pretty strong swimmer. His dad had taken him regularly to Warrender Park baths in Edinburgh, where he learned to swim. It wasn't the water; it was the temperature – the pool was ice cold. The brothers didn't seem to mind but as DJ walked towards them, he shivered like mad.

"Come on DJ. Dive. You're like an old woman there," laughed John.

With the water above his knees, DJ took a deep breath, about to take the plunge, when he saw the black-haired boy stare up at him. A hand grabbed his ankle and pulled. He fell forward, hitting the water with a splash; the air sucked from his lungs as he disappeared beneath the surface. It was totally freezing, his head and ears nipped. He opened his eyes, seeing the brothers' white legs – he swam towards them. The black-haired boy was between John's legs – staring right at him. White eyeballs like headlights. Petrified, he surfaced, air sucked back into his lungs.

"I saw somebody. Somebody's in the water John, behind you. Someone's behind you," he screamed.

The brothers laughed.

"I saw the black-haired boy in the water behind John...Seriously."

John saw he wasn't joking and dropped beneath the surface, followed by James. DJ joined them, all eyes open. Apart from riverbed rocks there was nothing else to be seen. They surfaced.

"There's nothing there DJ," said John.

"Didn't even see a fish," James shrugged.

"I bloody saw something. I'm serious."

James filled his mouth with water, spraying it on DJ's face.

"Did you see that," he laughed, swimming to the waterfall.

DJ and John swam after him – all three bodies treaded water under nature's shower. Here the pool was at its deepest and it's where John said you could find plenty of fish. Gallons of freezing hill water bounced off their white bodies, talk about refreshing – it was fridge freezing. John disappeared, swimming below DJ and grabbing at his feet. DJ sunk towards his pal and swam after him. For a good twenty minutes they splashed about and thankfully the black-haired boy was nowhere to be seen.

After their dip they sat on the riverbank – sun drying.

"Boys what is it with me seeing the black-haired boy? Ever since we went inside Castledawn I'm seeing him in my dreams, seeing him in the water. What's going on?"

"Sometimes the ripple of a river can play tricks on your eyes, DJ," said John.

"But he looked so real, I even saw him at the tobar. It's creepy."

"How old is he?" James asked.

"Eh... I didn't ask, obviously," smiled DJ sarcastically.

"Very funny. So funny I forgot to laugh. How old does he look?"

"Don't know. Maybe six or seven, Black hair and his eyes – all white. He looks at me like he wants to say something. No words come out just dark gunk like he's been eating bog mud."

"It's strange right enough, but we were with you, and we've seen nothing, no dreams or visions...nothing!" said John.

"Are you sure DJ? I mean are you really sure? Maybe you're having a daymare?' suggested a laughing James.

"Daymare? What? Can you have a nightmare during the day...? When you're awake?"

"Don't know. Maybe."

Once suitably dry, they dressed. The peat in the water had left them looking like they had a suntan. All three were starving and wanted to get home quick for their dinner. From the top of Totescore they raced. The finishing line being the road sign at the end of the boys' road. John won. John always won, his legs were the strongest and the longest. DJ came second. Saying his cheerios he freewheeled home, waving at Miss Murchison in the passing.

At dinner DJ got stuck into his food. Boiled potatoes and boiled ham slices with green peas. Catriona was beside him, and he attempted to feed her – she wasn't keen on anything but the peas, which was a first, she usually hated anything green. He did get a wee bit of ham in her mouth, but she spat it out after a couple of chews. Bess was on hand to lick up the mess. Catriona drank all her milk and DJ praised her, saying she would grow up big and strong like him. She laughed, milk dribbling from the corner of her mouth onto her Banana Splits bib.

After the dishes, the three of them sat outside – his mum on the sleeper, and DJ playing with Catriona on the lawn. It was a warm evening; a sea breeze kept the dreaded midges away. DJ stretched out on the grass, staring at the light blue sky. The sun edged westward and as it moved, it was followed by white puff-ball clouds. He thought about the black-haired boy. Maybe he was going mad. Maybe he was having a daymare. So deep in thought he didn't hear his mum talking to him.

"DJ. DJ... Are you listening?"

'Sorry mum. Miles away. What did you say?"

"I said I'm working tomorrow, so I expect your chores to be done. Don't want you disappearing with your friends and leaving your sister with Maggie all day. Maggie's busy too you know."

"Aye mum, sure. Don't worry."

He knew full well he'd be leaving Catriona with Maggie for at least a few hours.

In bed he could hardly keep his eyes open. His Commando book slipped from his hands, and he surrendered to sleep. He woke up on the bed in Castledawn. The fire roared and sparked. How did he get here? Outside the wind was blowing a gale, driving rain into the window with rat-a-tat, bullet like. He was at the window, looking out. Beneath him, a black horse-drawn carriage with lights either side of the driver's seat. The rain bounced off the backs of the shiny ebony horses, steam puffed from their noses. It looked like something you'd see in a Dickens movie. He couldn't tell if anyone was sitting in the carriage. What if he went down to have a look? He wanted to, but he was drawn to the bathroom, no control of his body and he passed through the open door. Sunny day bright and white as white could be. The tub – he didn't want to look, he knew what was there, he had no choice. A puppet on a string. Pushed against the bath, all his strength used. Nothing could stop the inevitable. Heart bursting, fear rising. The black-haired boy waited. Looked like he was sleeping. His eyes, ghost white and wide. Head rising, mouth open – an outpouring of a foul mix mulch. His hand grabbed DJ's wrist. DJ pulled away, hard, but the boy's grip was vice tight. A slow-motion movie – the ghastly porridge pouring from his mouth and nose.

"Find me."

DJ woke up, the room was stifling hot, he was crying, sweating too. He sat on the edge of the bed. Contemplating going downstairs to his sleeping mum, he didn't want to tell her about his dreams, she'd be too worried. He opened the skylight, a cooling air, he lay on top of the bed. Eyes open wide, he planned to stay awake until he heard his mum getting up.

"DJ. Time to get up darling," his mum, shouting from the foot of the stairs.

His attempt to stay awake had failed, he stared at the ceiling. Fear remained in his chest, the sound of his mum talking to Catriona made him less frightened.

Chapter 13

After his mum left for work, DJ and Catriona washed the breakfast bowls, Catriona took great delight in standing on the wooden stool and soaping the dishes before scrubbing them. DJ, at her side, dishcloth in hand, wiping off the foam and placing the dishes on the rack. Chores done he took his sister to Norman and Maggie's and although it was early, the sun above the Linicro rocks indicated it was going to be another scorcher. Perfect mucking about weather.

Maggie was in the kitchen, pottering about, DJ deposited Catriona and went out back to find Norman. He was dying to ask him about Castledawn and the folk who'd lived there. The tractor shed was open, and he could hear the rattle of tools. Norman was working on an old David Brown 990 tractor he was restoring. He had a new Massey Ferguson 565, but wanted to get the David Brown up and running, just for show and for fun. DJ admired the red and yellow beast, Norman stood polishing newly fitted headlamps on either side of the glossy red bonnet. The lights looked like eyeballs on a slug, a giant red slug.

"What do you think, boy? She's a beauty, eh?"

"She sure is. Any chance of getting a shot when you get her going?"

Norman laughed.

"She's running just fine. Just a few more things to pretty her up and she'll be ready. Do you think you're man enough to drive her?"

"Aye. Easy peasey," smiled DJ.

"Och, well you never know boy. You never know."

"Norman, what do you know about the folk who lived in Castledawn?"

"Castledawn eh."

"It such a beautiful building and I wondered why it was left to wrack and ruin."

"Aye you're right there boy, you're right there. It was a fine-looking house in its day. Should never have been built on Skye though. Not so close to the shore anyways. It's the salt you see, eats away at that Edinburgh sandstone."

"So? Do you know anything about its owners?"

'Och, that was a wee bit before my time, but there was a family there right enough. Lived there up until after the war.'

'What happened to them?'

'Well… If I remember rightly, they left after one of their children died. Went back to Edinburgh I believe. Relatives of the original owner, I think. The one who built the place. A banker or a lawyer so I heard. When he died, the house lay empty for years, then a family came to live there."

"What happened to the boy? Do you know? How old was he?"

'I don't remember exactly, but he was older than myself. Maybe around six or seven. A sickly boy so I was told. I only saw him once. They had a big car. Unusual for here. The boy was sitting in the back. I remember thinking he looked awfy pale. Like he never saw a bit of sun. Didn't see him again but I remember he had sisters, twins about my age."

"What colour of hair did he have?"

DJ's brain, turning to the boy in his dreams.

"Och... Now you're asking. Why are you so interested?"

'Don't know. Just wondered that's all. It's big building. I'm surprised nobody ever bought it."

"I heard it belongs to a bank in Edinburgh. The boy had dark hair, maybe black or brown. Och it was such a long time ago DJ, my memory isn't that good. You know who you could ask? Old Miss Murchison, she worked there as a housekeeper."

"Really?"

"Aye boy when she was young. Ask her she'll know more than me."

DJ would need to check if the old girl had any odd jobs needing done. He could ask her about Castledawn too, say it was for a school project. He had almost saved enough for his new bike, and he was desperate to get rid of his Jeep, although it had done him proud, his legs were stretching, and he needed something bigger, something sportier.

After a quick check on Catriona, he told Maggie he was off to meet the boys. Luckily, Maggie loved his sister and loved looking after her, too. He jumped on his bike and cycled towards Totescore. Miss Murchison was at her door. DJ stopped and asked if she needed any work done. She said she'd a big job for him and how did he feel about doing some painting? Might take a day or two she said. Painting was no problem for him, a picture of his dream bike floated in his mind. He'd do anything if it meant he'd have enough money to make his dream come true. Pedalling to his pals he wondered what needed painting? A day or two she said – definitely be a tenner in it for sure.

John and James were at the end of their road.

"Where to boys?" asked DJ.

"Can't stay too long. We have to weed the potatoes. Pretty bloody boring, no choice though. Want to go to the fank?"

Totescore fank was fine for DJ. Uphill, but not too far. They raced past the quarry and puffed past the second Totescore Road, sweat ran down their foreheads. At the top of the road, a cooling wind ran off the hill.

The Totescore fank was nothing like its Linicro counterpart. It was a collection of small concrete sheep pens with a fenced grazing field at the side. They liked to hang out there though, it was close to the road so they could watch the comings and goings of the locals and do a bit of tourist car spotting.

At the dipper, they threw stones into the stinky grey water.

"What about a trip to the pier tomorrow?" said James.

"Aye. Brilliant we can do a bit of line fishing," DJ said excitedly.

"Sounds like plan," agreed John.

The brothers climbed the wall of the loading pen and perched like freaky man crows. DJ, bored by his stone throwing climbed the lip of the concrete dipper. Jumping across the scummy sheep bath, he caught a glimpse of the black-haired boy, floating, staring – white eyes bright against the grey. He lost his footing, one leg on the opposite lip, the other, ankle deep in sheep dip – he almost toppled backwards into the murky mess. Wet leg up, he hopped clear of the dipper's depths. Frightened, he looked into the dipper, the cheerless grey and his own reflection was all he saw.

"Right... Don't laugh... I just saw the black-haired boy again. Floating in the dipper. Staring up at me."

The brothers jumped the wall and climbed the dipper, two set of legs spread-eagled either side of the concrete bath. They looked down. Saw nothing but their wavy reflections.

"You saw yourself," said James.

"Was it incredibly scary and ugly? Then it definitely was you," laughed John.

'Ha ha! Funny. I'm telling you. I saw him."

"We believe you," John assured him.

"Thousands wouldn't," James laughed.

"I saw him, a clear as I see you two."

"Seriously boy, we believe," said John, meaning it.

"And another thing, I forgot to tell you...Last night, in my dream the black-haired boy spoke to me."

"What did he say?" John asked.

"Find me. He said find me. Strange!"

"What does that even mean?" asked James.

"Don't know... Anyway... Listen, I need to get back. I'm supposed to be looking after Catriona."

DJ was less scared but still a bit shaky.

They jumped their bikes and raced down the road – John won, as usual.

"Fishing tomorrow?" John asked.

"Suppose so," replied DJ. "What time?"

"Meet us here at one... And listen. We believe you DJ. If you say you saw the boy, then you saw the boy.

We need to figure out who he is and why it's only you that's seeing him."

"OK, OK. It's eerie and a bit scary."

"Don't worry boy," smiled John. "You've got us."

They took off home and DJ headed to Maggie's, feeling a wee bit better. Miss Murchison waved him to stop, she wanted to talk more about the painting job.

"Do you think you can manage, DJ? How's your painting skills?"

Maybe she was having second thoughts and that he wasn't up for the work.

"Pretty good," he lied.

"I'll be needing my guttering and drainpipes done. Front and back. Do you think you can do it, son?"

"No bother," he said with an overconfident grin. "When?"

"What about tomorrow, if it's dry?"

"Oh... Can't do tomorrow... Fishing trip planned. What about the day after? Saturday?"

"Aye, OK son. That'll be grand."

After collecting Catriona, they sat out on the lawn, playing. Rough and tumble, where he rolled her about and flipped her in the air – she couldn't stop laughing. He laughed too. Bess looked on wondering what all the fuss was about. They were still outside when his mum got back from work. Parking inside the gate, DJ ran to close it, Catriona ran to her mum, hugging her legs.

"Hey you two. Miss me? DJ be a darling take the shopping to the kitchen, please."

Grumpy faced, he did what he was told. She stopped him.

"What no kiss?"

With a loud sigh he pecked her cheek.

In the kitchen, DJ put the shopping away and his mum prepared dinner. Catriona sat on the floor talking to somebody, probably her dolls.

"Mummy, Daddy's here," she said without looking up.

"That's right, darling. Daddy's always here, watching over us from heaven."

Catriona often said stuff like that.

With dinner finished he and his mum washed up. She washed; DJ dried.

"So how was your day? I take it by the way you wolfed down your dinner, you were busy?"

"Not really. We were at the fank. Totescore fank. Sitting around. Tomorrow we're going to Uig pier, fishing. Should be fun."

"Well, just be careful. Don't want you or your friends falling in the sea."

"Mum... Never going to happen and even if it did, we can swim."

"Just be careful anyway."

"Sure mum."

He stayed up late reading his old Action comics – his favourites, he'd kept every issue from the year before. In Edinburgh his mum wasn't keen on him reading them because of the goriness – that's why he loved them. After much discussion she acquiesced, allowing him to buy it with his pocket money. The gore DJ enjoyed was the comics' downfall. Parents complained, it even got a mention in Parliament and was featured on John Craven's Newsround. The stories were toned down with most of the blood and guts stuff removed. DJ stopped buying it and was glad he'd kept the old issues. Hookjaw,

Dredger and Death Game 1999 were his favourites. He read till the candle was spent. His eyelids were heavy, he tried his best to keep them open, eventually succumbing to sleep.

He didn't dream of Castledawn. He dreamt he was at Edinburgh Zoo with his dad. Laughing and having fun. They ate Wall's Vanilla ice-cream and shared a can of Pepsi. DJ felt incredibly happy.

"Remember DJ. I'm always here," said his dad.

Chapter 14

DJ woke to the sound of the kitchen door closing. He stared at the ceiling, in the corner by the window was a big black and white spider. Its silver spun web shimmered in the sunlight. He watched it go about its business and thought about his dad. His dream left him feeling incredibly joyful, and he was glad the black-haired boy hadn't made an appearance. Before getting up he named the spider Peter, after Spiderman. He smiled at that.

Starving, he scoffed his porridge, his mum added a teaspoon of syrup and he liked to mix it in the bowl along with milk.

"What do you tearaways have planned for today darling?"

"Fishing, remember?" he replied with a mouthful of porridge.

"Are you going to tell me where?" she asked. "Or is it a secret?"

"Uig... At the pier. Told you already."

"Really? Must have slipped my mind. You will be careful, won't you?"

He gave her a look; she reached over and ruffled his hair.

"I know. I know. You're a good swimmer and all that. I'm your mum darling. It's my job to worry."

After his chores he readied his fishing gear, not that there was much to get ready. He'd found an enamel First Aid box in the shed which he'd cleaned up, polishing away the rust. Inside, his meagre supply of hooks, small lead weights and a spinning lure Norman had given him. His fishing line was wrapped around a tree branch which he had cut from one of Norman's trees. With his dad's pen knife, he'd stripped away the bark, cut it to a short length and twisted the gut which was held in place by a small steel hook. He stuffed everything into his Adidas bag along with a packed lunch – milk loaf cheese sandwiches and a packet of Yoyo's, his mum's treat. Mint, of course. When he saw the green foil-wrapped chocolate biscuits, he wanted to tell her he loved her, but he didn't, he felt shy. Not only did he love her, he admired how brave and tough she was and one day he'd find the right words to say to her.

Rain clouds had crept over from Harris and the sky darkened – it was warm, though. Before leaving, he played hide and seek, with Catriona, hiding at the side of the house, never too far and he always let her win. She was happy about that.

At eleven he slung his bag across his shoulder, jumped his bike and was off up the road. In the distance, across the fields he could see two black shapes moving fast up the Totescore Road. He stopped at Miss Murchison's, knocking on her door.

"Hi Miss Murchison," he said, opening her living room door.

She was sitting by the window darning thick woollen socks, a cup of tea sat steaming on the corner of the mantelpiece.

"Morning DJ," she said. Not looking up.

"Morning, just wanted to check about tomorrow. You still want me to come?"

"Oh aye, son. That I do. That I do. Got new paint delivered yesterday from Uig. Even bought you a new brush," she smiled.

"OK, great. How's nine o'clock?"

"Aye boy. That'll be grand. That'll be grand."

"Miss Murchison, Norman told me you worked at Castledawn House. Is that right?'

"That I did. A good few years. Housekeeping and such. Oh, it was a grand place at one time."

"I'd like to know more about it, if you don't mind. If you remember, that is?"

"Oh, I remember alright. I might be old, but my faculties are intact," she smiled.

"Great. OK. Look forward to hearing your stories. Better be off. We're going fishing at the pier. I will see you tomorrow."

"Fishing, is it? OK, son. I think I have a photograph or two taken at Castledawn. Black and white in them days. I will look them out."

"Wow. That'd be brilliant. OK. Bye now."

"Cheery."

DJ was excited to tell the brothers about the photographs. The boys were waiting, James leaned against the road sign. John was looking out to sea. A black spot moving along the Waternish coast told him the ferry was coming to Uig. It would be fun to watch *the Hebrides* load and unload cars – you could laugh at the tourists.

Out of puff they made it to the top of Totescore before DJ told them about Miss Murchison's photographs. John was more interested than James. They raced towards to the top of Uig. Descending into the village like three bullets, rounding the hairpin bend they turned off on to the Idrigill Road with its dips and curves. Soon they were at the pier road.

Cars queued, waiting the ferry's arrival. The boys waved at the smiling tourists who happily waved back. The *Heb* rounded Idrigal Point, and they were at the end of the pier to see the boat chug towards them. DJ had seen the ferry berth many times – it still made him excited. The red, black, and white of Caledonian Macbrayne's *Pride of the Minch* was beautiful, to him it looked like a luxury cruise ship. He'd only ever been on the car ferry at Kyle and that was hardly what you'd call fancy. The *MV Hebrides'* engines roared in reverse. Sea water spumed and splashed. Pier men waited for boatmen to throw across thick sea-soaked ropes – the ferry inched closer, loud gurgling noises bubbled up beneath her. Seagulls flew overhead, squawking and squealing. The ropes were tossed from the deck, caught by the pier men who wrapped them round black metal bollards. The boat came to a halt, bashing up against black tyres stuck to the pier's edge.

By the time the cars and buses had offloaded, the boys had gone to their fishing spot. At the side of the pier, concrete steps descended into the bay, this is where local fishermen landed their catch – the perfect spot to do line fishing. The tide was out, but soon would turn; it wouldn't affect the fishing, as the water rose, they'd climb back up the steps. To keep them from splashing into the sea was a rusty handrail, a wee bit shoogly it was in dire need of replacement.

DJ loved fishing here – most of the time they didn't catch much other than the occasional bodach ruadh, a small red and brown fish which they'd throw back into the bay. The boys' father said these wee fish tasted good fried. DJ had never tried, he couldn't see the point – they were so small with hardly any meat on them. With the low tide, they stood on the lowest landing. This far down you had to be very careful, the concrete was green and slimy and incredibly slippery. One time DJ almost skated off into the water, luckily John's big hand saved him.

James and DJ unpacked their lines. John hunted for bait. White and grey shelled limpets clung to the steps, perfect bait. Skill was needed to detach them from the concrete, the secret was a quick kick, not too hard or you'd boot them into the water. Not too soft either, they'd suck onto the concrete really hard, making them difficult to remove in one piece, shells would shatter, and the insides became a gooey mess. Once dislodged, John would scoop out the squelchy innards with his thumb – he'd use his pen knife to cut the unfortunate creature into small pieces, ready for baiting the hooks. DJ remembered the first time they came down here. A winter Saturday, no tourists just the odd fisherman and John forgot to bring his knife. He used his teeth to bite into the limpet's leathery flesh, ripping off pieces for their hooks. DJ thought it was disgusting, it was also pretty cool. After some coaxing he tried it himself – eyes closed, he bit into the limpet – tasted like salty chewing gum. It didn't taste too bad.

Now, he was a limpet booting expert – a couple of kicks dislodged two from the steps. The third, ended up in the bay, a miss-kick. James kicked at one and each of them set about scooping the leathery insides with their thumbs. John's pen knife cut the shellfish into small bits. With lines at the ready, they hooked pieces of meat and dropped them into the water. Standing side by side, they leaned over the handrail trying to attract a bite. The bay water, coloured lime green and clear, patches of white sea-bed sand surrounded by barnacle encrusted rocks. There wasn't an abundance of fish, maybe the ferry berthing scared them off. Fishing was a waiting game – a game difficult for impatient teenagers to play. Looking at the pier legs, DJ wondered if the metal underneath the crustations was rusty and how do they replace rusty legs?

"Boys, check it out."

James pointed to a group of fish that had turned up – not what you'd call huge. Their hooks, far too big for such tiny-mouthed creatures – it wasn't impossible to hook one, though. The trick was to give the line a good yank when they came close to nibble the limpet meat, the barb could go anywhere, though, not necessarily in the mouth. There was no talking – too busy concentrating. A competition unsaid – who'd be the first to land a fish, each boy wanting to win. DJ had a wee bodach swim around his hook, definitely interested. He waited and waited. It darted around, took a nibble, then another, when it came for a third bite, he pulled the line hard... Nothing... The fish swam off... Fast.

"Woo hoo!" cried James.

Smiling, he twisted his line round the wooden handle, reeling it in as quickly as he could. On the end of the line, a small, squirming red and brown fish.

"I'm the king, I'm the fishing king," he shouted.

"It huge," laughed John.

"It's a whale," chimed DJ.

"You're just jealous," James smiled. A look of satisfaction on his face.

The fish flapped in his palm, he gently unhooked it and, holding it by the tail, proudly showed it off as if some invisible cameraman was about to take a photo.

"Wanna a kiss it DJ?"

"Kiss my bum."

James dropped it into the water, it didn't hang around, disappearing into the bay. Baiting his hook and grinning, he lowered his line, satisfied knowing he had won the competition. DJ was next to land a fish, James argued with him about whose was bigger. John hooked one, pulled it up and his fish was obviously the biggest of the three. Big smile, he threw it back.

They carried on fishing until after the ferry had left for Stornoway, catching and releasing, arguing about fish size and climbing step by step to escape the incoming tide. Hungry, they packed up their gear and sat at the end of the pier, legs dangling over the water as they ate cheese sandwiches and chocolate biscuits. Across the bay stood the tall cliffs of Earlish. DJ had wanted to go there for ages, walk close to the edge, but his mum would go mental if she found out and from the village, it was a pretty steep hill to cycle up, One day, maybe.

The sky lightened; patches of blue peeped through the grey. Bellies full, they walked their bikes along the pier, cars gathered outside Macbrayne's office, booked on the evening ferry to Castlebay. Their walk continued the length of Idrigill road, at the bottom of the bealach path James suggested pushing the bikes up the steep shortcut.

"Come on. It will be a laugh and save time," he smiled.

DJ and John agreed. Not because they thought it would be quicker, but because they thought it would be funny. The hill path was incredibly steep, most of it hidden under bracken and weeds. They set off, pushing the bikes as best they could – James led, DJ was in the middle with John behind him urging them to move faster. Halfway up, they took a breather.

"This was a terrible idea," DJ said, red faced and sweaty.

"What? Not strong enough boy?" said John, also red faced.

"Stronger than I look," he smiled, passing James who was sat puffing on the grass.

At the top of the bealach, the wind was breezy and cool – they agreed never to take a shortcut again, it was easier, and less tiring on the legs to cycle round the hairpin bend.

Before leaving DJ at the top of their road an arrangement was made to meet at Stonegate after DJ finished Miss Murchison's painting job.

At home, DJ played with Catriona, he told her he'd caught a shark, but it had got away. She believed him.

Chapter 15

The black-haired boy appeared in DJ's dreams, waking him early – heart pounding and a fist of fear balled in his chest. His mum was leaving for work and issued him with the usual instructions. She knew he'd be at Miss Murchison's most of the day and Maggie would look after his sister.

He finished his porridge and woke Catriona who was in a bad mood and wanted her mum but settled for a chocolate-covered digestive. After a quick wash with her favourite flannel, he dressed her and deposited her in Maggie's kitchen. Outside Miss Murchison's front door, stood a shiny new aluminium step ladder and two tins of grey paint. As promised, there were two new paint brushes. He knocked her door.

"Morning Miss Murchison."

"Morning DJ. Come away in boy. Sit yourself down. You want a wee cup of tea before you start?"

He didn't, but he did want to know about Castledawn.

"Aye. Two sugars and milk, please."

He sat at the small dining table in the corner of her small living room.

"So, how's your mammy and that wee Catriona?"

"They're OK. Catriona is with Maggie. Mum's at work today."

"Oh, that's good. That's good son."

She handed him a mug of tea. The skin on her hands resembled well-worn leather. She might be old, but she looked pretty tough.

"How was your fishing trip with the tearaway brothers? Catch anything big?"

"Nothing big at all. Just wee tiddlers."

"Maybe the bait, son. Maybe the bait."

"We used limpet meat."

"Limpet meat, was it? My father was a fisherman. Oh aye. He fished all over. Even in America. According to him the best bait was bloodworms – he said you could catch anything with them."

"Bloodworms?' What are they?"

"Oh, laddie. Have you never seen a bloodworm?"

Never seen? He'd never even heard of such a creature.

"Don't think so."

"Och, they used to bring them over in barrows of earth. From the east coast of America, you see. Aye that's what they did. Many a fisherman on Skye's used a bloodworm – big red and juicy, fish love them son."

"What... You can find them here... In Linicro?"

"Aye, I'm sure you can. Just have to dig in the right places," she smiled.

DJ didn't believe the old girl. Surely, she was kidding him on, but he went along with it.

"I'll definitely look for them next time we're going fishing,"

"Just be careful the blighters don't bite you. They've fangs you know. Four of them. Made of metal so they say. Can give you a right good nip."

Now he knew she was pulling his leg.

"Well, I'll watch out for their teeth if I ever find one," smiled DJ.

"So, you'll be wanting to know about Castledawn, eh?"

"Whatever you can remember. Might use it for a school project," he lied.

"Och, school, is it? I don't know about that, but I'll tell you what I remember. It was ever so long ago."

She told him she'd worked in Castledawn House as a housekeeper. She was eighteen. The family that lived there were relatives of the gentleman who had built the house. She thought they were his brother's grandchildren. A family of four from Edinburgh, they used Castledawn as a summer house and occasionally spent Christmas there. When the war began, the father went to France and was killed. His wife and children never returned to Skye. The house was owned by a private bank run by the owner's family. They tried to sell it but couldn't find a buyer. She'd heard someone wanted to turn it into a guest house but that fell through. The private bank went bankrupt, and the house transferred to another bank who she thinks still owns it. They let it go to wrack and ruin.

"Did anything bad ever happen there?"

"What do you mean?"

"I don't know. Like, did anybody die or something?"

"Oh laddie, it's strange you should ask that. The folk I worked for had three children two girls, Bernadette and Euphemia. They were twins, identical, very hard to tell who was who. I'd make one wear a ponytail and the other wear pigtails just so I could tell them apart. They had an older brother, Montgomery, Monty, we called him. The laddie was asthmatic they said, always poorly. One summer he had a bad attack and they lost him. Very sad. Such a shame. I hear tell the original owner's wife died there too, some strange illness. That's why they built the house in the first place, she'd been ill in Edinburgh and the doctors there said good country air and a sea breeze would help her. I don't know if it did, but she died, and the rumour was her husband died not too long after her. A broken heart they said."

"Did you hear any ghost stories when you worked there?"

"Oh, DJ, Skye's full of ghost stories. Especially ghosts that live in old houses," she smiled.

"Aye but were there any ghosts there. Like, in the house?'

"Not that I know of. When the house was empty, the locals told the children it was haunted. You know, to keep them away from the place."

"You didn't hear or see anything when you worked there?"

"No son. Not a thing. It was a beautiful house. A happy house. Up until the boy died and the war started."

"OK. Thanks. It's an interesting place. Looks like some of the big houses in Edinburgh. Nothing like a Skye house."

"Your right there DJ. Maybe the owner wanted a wee bit of Edinburgh on Skye, eh? I will look out the photos I promised."

After one last gulp of tea, he went outside to prepare the paint and stuff. The house was small, smaller than his, the guttering and drainpipes would be easy to paint but they needed a good clean first. They old girl brought out a brush and a bucket of soapy water. There was a garden trowel for scraping gutter gunk. Rolling up his sleeves, he got on with it. The stepladder used for the guttering was a wee bit shoogly, but he managed. After scrubbing and scraping away the dirt, he set about painting. The drainpipes first. He popped open the paint tin lid with the trowel, rounding behind the house and he snapped a twig from a tree. The grey paint was thick and smelly, he used the twig to give it a good stir. Satisfied with its consistency, he grabbed the paint pot and started painting. DJ enjoyed painting, and this job required little finesse. Dabbing the brush in the pot, he slapped on the paint, stroking up and down, smoothing it out as much as he could. It was non-drip stuff, so it wasn't too messy. The guttering had to be painted inside and out. A thick coat of paint protected the metal from the rust-producing Skye weather. He could've done a better job of cleaning the guttering, but what Miss Murchison couldn't see wouldn't hurt her. The house was clad in corrugated iron sheets and unlike the rusty red of the shepherd's cottage it was painted a light grey. The paint DJ used was a lot darker. Maybe one day she'd get him to paint the whole house – that was a big job. He'd definitely need help from his Totescore pals.

By the time he finished he was sweaty, and his mouth was desert dry. Miss Murchison gave him a glass of Robinson's lemon barley which he finished in one long glug. In the shed he found turps and a plastic bowl, he let the brushes soak whilst he tidied up. Both brushes got a final rinse under the outside water tap, so did his hands. The old lady came out and inspected his handiwork.

"Och, you've done a grand job there DJ. A grand job indeed."

She produced her purse, pulling out a ten-pound note. She smiled and handed it to him.

"Are you sure Miss Murchison? Five pounds would be more than enough."

"Oh, you're a good laddie. No. You did a fine job, and you deserve it."

"Thank you. I'm saving for a new bike. My old one's getting small for me."

"A new bike, is it? Well, we will have to see about getting you more work before the school starts, eh? Oh... Here... nearly forgot I found this photo of me and the girls from Castledawn. I was young once."

The black and white photo showed a huge car, parked in front of Castledawn, standing beside it, two girls in fancy dresses – blonde hair and pigtails. They were like carbon copies. Beside them stood a tall girl wearing a pinney and a stern look. DJ glanced at Miss Murchison, then back at the photo. She must've shrunk in her old age.

"You're right about the girls – they look the exact same to me," he said.

"Aye. That they were. Bernadette and Euphemia. I think they would've been four or five in that picture. I thought I had a photo of Monty, but I couldn't find it. You can keep that one if you like. I have another, framed and hanging on the bedroom wall."

"Are sure? Can't wait to show to the boys."

"Aye son, you take it. It's not seen the light of day for many a year."

"Great. Thank you so much for this and the money,"

"Get away with yourself. You did a grand job laddie."

***

DJ sat in the living room, flicking through a comic with Catriona sat at his feet. Under the table, Bess was crunching on an old soup bone. The sound of the Beetle announced his mum was home.

"How are my darlings? Did you miss me?"

"Miss you mummy. Miss you," shouted a smiling Catriona.

"Go get the shopping darling. Please."

With a sigh, DJ did what he was told.

At dinner he showed the Castledawn photo to his mum and couldn't wait to show it to John and James. Once finished doing the dishes he got on his bike and puffed his way to Totescore. The afternoon grey had cleared, and a few fluffy clouds floated over from Waternish. A still Minch, resembling an extra-large pane of glass, twinkled in the evening sun. He bumped down the mud track that led to the ruins of Stonegate cottage. The boys sat outside the old shed. James was all smiles, John flicked through a dog-eared Commando comic book.

"See what I got from old Miss Murchison," said DJ, excited as anything.

"What? Did she give you a photo of herself that you could put by your bed and kiss every night?" laughed James puckering his lips and kissing the air.

"Very funny. Remind me to laugh."

He handed the photo to John.

"The two lassies were twins. And that's Miss Murchison beside them. Looks a bit different back then, eh?" said DJ.

"What, do you fancy her?" said James, kissing the air again.

"Check the front of the house, quite a bit different from how it looks now. What do you think?"

"Aye, it's a nice photo right enough," said John, handing it to his brother.

"How old were the lassies?" James asked.

"Four or five but get this, they had a brother a few years older. He died in the house, asthma or something."

"Do you think he's the boy in your dreams?" asked John.

"Who else could it be?"

"Creepy." said James.

For an hour they sat on the hill throwing stones into the middle of the roofless cottage. Inside the ruin was a mass of green, mostly stinging nettles and thistles – slap bang in the middle was a patch of purple foxgloves stretching towards the sky. Beauty and the beast thought DJ.

***

When he got home, his mum was braiding Catriona's hair and listening to the radio. He sat with them for a while, playing with his sister, distracting her from hair-pulling hands. In bed he read a Commando comic book called The Long Trek but found it hard to concentrate. His mind wandered towards Castledawn and the boy who died, Was he the black-haired boy in the bath? He stared at the photo, looking for answers to an unknown question and he saw something he hadn't noticed before. Behind the twins in one of the upstairs windows was the silhouette of a body – someone small by the looks of it. Peeping out from behind the curtains. There was no detail in the grainy picture, but it definitely was someone. Maybe the brother? But wasn't he dead? The photo could've been taken before he died. He'd have to check with Miss Murchison.

Castledawn and the black-haired boy haunted his dreams once more.

Chapter 16

It was early evening, DJ sat in the smiddy waiting. John Travolta and Olivia Newton John sang 'You're the one that I want' through the medium wave crackle – he joined in with the 'ooh ooh ooh,' chorus. Linicro had baked all day in the summer sun, and it was roasting under the smiddy's corrugated roof. Dust floated in the air and bars of sunlight poked through the roof, making the dust shimmer. The window and the holey roof allowed air to circulate, a light Minch breeze blew through and up and out. John's smiling face appeared at the window, he climbed through, James was behind him.

"I need to show you something," said DJ. Holding the black and white photo.

"What now?" grinned James. "More photos of your new girlfriend?"

"Yeah, yeah. Look... I noticed this last night."

Six eyes stared at the picture.

"You noticed what?" asked John.

DJ pointed to the black shape in the upstairs window.

"See? Somebody's there, looking out the window. Small by the looks of it, definitely not an adult."

"Probably the brother." John stared into the photo.

"Aye, it's the brother, too sick to have his photo taken," James agreed.

"Need to ask Miss Murchison when it was taken," said DJ.

"What do you mean?" James asked.

"Was it before or after the boy died? I'm sure it's after, I remember her saying something about it."

"Come on then, let's go ask," said John.

Heading to the quarry, they stopped at Miss Murchison's. The old girl was at her door enjoying the evening air.

"Och, its three handsome gentlemen callers," she smiled.

"Hi Miss Murchison," they said together.

'How's your mother and father, John?"

"Aye. They're fine, thanks. How are you?"

"Grand laddie. Just grand."

"Don't mean to bother you, but we wanted to ask about the photo you gave me," said DJ.

"Oh, right… Well… What is it you want to know?"

"Eh… Do you know if it was taken before or after the boy died? Monty?"

"Oh… I see… Well, if I remember rightly, it was after the poor laddie passed away."

"Really?"

"Oh, aye. Monty died the previous year I believe; summer, I'm sure. Why are you asking?"

"No reason. I was telling the boys what you told me about Castledawn."

"It was a grand place right enough. Not the same though, after the boy died. Sad place after that."

"Thanks Miss Murchison… Anyway…Sorry to bother you. We'll be off. Let me know if you need any jobs done."

"Aye boy. I will indeed. Nice to see the township tearaways," she laughed.

On the road to the quarry, all three were silent. Thinking. Wondering who it was at the window and did he have anything to do with DJ's dreams.

Sitting on the grass by the quarry's long red gate, they studied the Castledawn picture.

"So, if the shadow at the window isn't the brother, who is it?" DJ asked.

"Good question," said John.

"Yes, but what's the answer?" James frowned.

"Right... Eh... Listen, I didn't want to say anything before, but something else has been happening," said DJ.

"What now?" said James.

"Well... Right... Don't laugh... I've been hearing a voice...Whispering my name! Started when I found the note from Cornelius Black. Sounded like my dad... I mean... Look... I don't know. I thought maybe it was just the wind or the pigeon that came flying out of the fireplace. Couple of days later I saw my dad standing outside the smiddy. I mean... Like... Just for a moment."

There was silence.

DJ's eyes looked towards the Minch – watching the *Hebrides* pass Kilbride on its way to Stornoway.

"Look, whatever's happening, it started when we went to Castledawn," said John.

"You're right there," James agreed.

"If we want answers, we have to go back," DJ looked from one to the other.

"Exactly what I was thinking."

"Oh what? Do we have to? Really? Man... Things are getting weird and creepy," said James.

"What? Are you scared of a wee ghost?" teased his brother.

"Aye. I am."

"Me too,' said DJ.

"Don't think we have choice. Maybe we'll find something we missed last time," said John. "Please tell me were not going to the creepy cellar," moaned his brother.

"Don't worry, boy. I'll hold your hand," DJ smiled.

"Suppose we can check the upstairs bathroom. See if DJ was right about the secret door," said James, trying to draw attention away from the cellar.

"We need to make a plan. A camping and Castledawn plan," said John.

They sat, discussing what to do – finally deciding to camp down at Duntulm the following weekend – this time they'd tell their folks. As long as they called home, they thought their folks would say yes. DJ wasn't sure about his mum – he'd do his best to persuade her. He didn't want to lie again.

It was eight o'clock when he said cheerio to the boys. On the way home he went over the conversation he'd have with his mum. Best thing to do was to ask straight away. Get it over and done with. He was more than a wee bit apprehensive when he opened the front door.

After filling the water buckets, he took a deep breath and came out with it. He was surprised by her reaction. She didn't even put up a fight. He promised to call her both nights and if there was an emergency they'd go to the Coastguard for help. With that said she was happy.

Castledawn dreams woke him up in the middle of the night. The boy's grip was tighter, his voice louder.

"Find me."

Chapter 17

The black-haired boy visited DJ's dreams all week. It scared him but he also felt excitement at the thought of finally getting some answers – he wasn't keen to go near water though, just in case the boy's eyes were staring.

The day before the trip something strange happened. His mum had asked him to clear the bothy on the croft of weeds and boulders, it wasn't a big space, but it took him all afternoon to finish. Norman would rebuild the walls and re-roof it with corrugated plastic sheets. DJ found a gate in the undergrowth; Norman could clean it up and give it a coat of paint ready for it to be the door of the new goat shed. DJ was still unconvinced about the goats, but his mum was excited, and he liked to see her happy – it made him happy. About to head to the house, he felt a hand on his shoulder. His heart stopped, his stomach dropped, and he jumped forward in terror. Nobody was behind him. A wind rolled down from the hill blowing through his hair and carrying his dad's voice.

"Be careful son."

His heart started and although scared, he felt comforted. Scared but not scared – a strange feeling to have. Was he going mad? No matter. If there were

Castledawn dreams woke him up in the middle of the night. The boy's grip was tighter, his voice louder.
"Find me."

Chapter 17

The black-haired boy visited DJ's dreams all week. It scared him but he also felt excitement at the thought of finally getting some answers – he wasn't keen to go near water though, just in case the boy's eyes were staring.

The day before the trip something strange happened. His mum had asked him to clear the bothy on the croft of weeds and boulders, it wasn't a big space, but it took him all afternoon to finish. Norman would rebuild the walls and re-roof it with corrugated plastic sheets. DJ found a gate in the undergrowth; Norman could clean it up and give it a coat of paint ready for it to be the door of the new goat shed. DJ was still unconvinced about the goats, but his mum was excited, and he liked to see her happy – it made him happy. About to head to the house, he felt a hand on his shoulder. His heart stopped, his stomach dropped, and he jumped forward in terror. Nobody was behind him. A wind rolled down from the hill blowing through his hair and carrying his dad's voice.

"Be careful son."

His heart started and although scared, he felt comforted. Scared but not scared – a strange feeling to have. Was he going mad? No matter. If there were answers to be found at Castledawn – tomorrow was the day they'd find them.

***

John and James arrived mid-afternoon. Linicro was enjoying the sun. The blue sky stretched way past the Harris hills with barely a cloud. At the gate they checked their supplies. John's jerry-rigged trailer stored all the gear and before they took off, DJ's mum reminded him about phoning and what to do in the event of an emergency. He nodded and smiled. The boys laughed.

"Did your mum pack your teddy this time," laughed James as they cycled down Linicro.

"She did," DJ smiled.

By the time they reached Kilmuir Post Office they were boiling hot and sweating like mad.

"Ice cream break," announced John.

Sitting against the whitewashed Post Office wall they silently enjoyed their Walls cooling treat. The Hungladder hill was ahead and in this heat it wouldn't be easy. Halfway to the top DJ gave up, and they walked the rest of the way – puffing hard. Wasn't too long before they crossed the cattle grid at the top and from there it was downhill all the way.

The good weather had brought the tourists out and many cars were on the road through Score. James took great delight at checking bumper stickers and announcing the country they were from. Three German cars, two Belgian and a fancy French Renault, full of smiling, waving tourists. At Duntulm Castle several cars were parked and folk were walking to and from the castle. At the camping spot, firewood was scavenged by DJ and James whilst John set about pitching the tent; he'd ordered them to fetch as much wood as they could carry. They were happy to let him do the boring work, as they walked the shore. The tide was out, revealing patches of black sand and green seaweed, surrounded by millions of ankle-breaking rocks. Where the grass met the shore was where you found the flotsam and jetsam, washed up by the high tide. Loads of wooden crates were strewn about, dumped either by local fishing boats or foreign trawlers that fished the Minch. The salt had turned the wood bone pale and brittle, very easy to break-up for firewood.

They sang Hotel California at the top of their lungs.

"Think we've got enough wood to burn for a week," said DJ.

"You can never have enough wood," James replied.

"Better get it up to the tent or you know who will complain."

"Aye. He likes to do that right enough," laughed James.

The boulder fire circle remained intact. From his bike trailer John produced an axe and began chopping kindling. Aided by scrunched up Press and Journal newspaper sheets the fire roared into life. It was far from cold, but the heat was needed for their baked beans and frankfurters dinner. DJ had the usual selection of cheese scones: treacle and plain. They were starving by early evening and wolfed down their hot food accompanied by a Fanta treat from DJ's mum. She liked to do things like that for him and his friends, even though she complained about fizzy drinks rotting teeth. She'd packed a box of McVitie's chocolate digestives too.

With full stomachs they sat staring into the fire. All thinking about Castledawn. Later, they went for a walk. Tourists were still out in force at the castle and as they passed the Coastguard's house, about to cut down the hill to the lochan, a car horn beeped at their back. It was Mr. Mackenzie in his blue and yellow Coastguard Land Rover. He stopped, rolling down the window he smiled.

"Alright boys? John how's that father of yours? Behaving himself?"

"Oh aye. You know him. He's fine thanks."

"Was that your tent I saw up the road a bit? Green one? Looks like an army tent?"

"It is. A cracker isn't it?" said James.

"That it is, boy. That it is. How long are you camping for?"

"Two nights," replied DJ.

"Two nights, is it? Awfy brave of you. Especially with all those ghosts in the castle," Mr Mackenzie smiled.

"Aye. We have invited them for a strupag* later," laughed James.

The Coastguard laughed too saying "Och... OK boys. I'd better get on. You'll be careful now, won't you? If you need anything, just give me a shout. If I'm not in, Morag's always here.

"Thanks Mr. Mackenzie."

He took off down the road to his front door. At the phone box they made their promised calls home. DJ first, then James. Walking back to the tent they sang Don't Cry for me Argentina even though they didn't know all the words.

---

* A cup of tea.

John threw more firewood on the fire and they sat watching the flames, listening to the wood crack and squeak. Although it was after eleven the sky wasn't dark – it was navy blue with a sprinkling of stars. Before bed, John doused the fire and they crawled into the tent – shoes off and into their sleeping bags. The brothers talked, DJ tried to listen, but his eyelids were heavy. Their voices drifted out of the tent, seaward and he fell fast asleep.

"DJ... DJ..."

DJ's eyes opened.

"DJ... DJ... Are you awake son?"

DJ's vision cleared and he was looking up at a familiar ceiling. He wasn't in the tent. He was in his Bruntsfield bedroom and sitting at the foot of his bed was his dad. Happiness coursed through his body.

"DJ... DJ... You have to help find him. Please find him."

His dad's mouth stayed closed, but his voice was clear as day.

"Find the black-haired boy son."

Eyes opened, DJ was in the tent between his two pals – both snoring. At times, when he'd dream about his dad, DJ would wake up feeling sad. Not today, today he felt a warm glow across his chest. It felt good, right. Felt like his dad's love. DJ allowed himself to enjoy the feeling, enjoy that wee moment wrapped in love.

Stuck between snorers, he couldn't get back to sleep. His thoughts wandered towards Claire Ross and the night they kissed. It had been at the school Christmas dance, a three-piece highland dance band providing the music. For the previous month all the first years had to endure

Scottish country dancing classes during PE. Everybody hated it. DJ said he hated it, but really, he didn't. He didn't mind because the girls PE class joined them, and he could see Claire. She lived down the Cuil road in Uig and he really fancied her. Claire was a sporty girl, fit and pleasing to look at in her gym stuff. They both shared a number of classes and DJ would take any opportunity to talk to her. He thought she liked him too, but he didn't know what to do about it. At the dance, when the band played the Grand Old Duke of York, he made sure he asked her to dance. Everyone knew this dance was one where you could get a kiss. Holding hands, him and Claire danced under a couple holding their arms in an arch shape and when they passed through, the couple's arms would drop, locking them together until they kissed. It was brilliant. Her lips were soft, and she smelled nice. It wasn't a long kiss, more a peck, but to DJ it was perfect. When the band called the last dance, a waltz, Claire surprised him by asking to dance. He was nervous as heck, putting his hands on her waist, her arms wrapped round his neck, and she pulled him close, DJ was in heaven. A couple of lassies were going round the dance floor with mistletoe, holding it above people's heads who then had to kiss. A wee sprig of mistletoe was held above DJ and Claire. He was almost shaking with nerves; Claire smiled, moving her lips towards him. They kissed until the band stopped playing. Afterwards, DJ stood in front of the school waiting for Norman to pick him up. Felt like he was floating on a cotton wool cloud. He could still feel Claire's lips. Over the last six months, he thought about that kiss a lot. He wanted to ask Claire to be his girlfriend but he lacked courage and confidence. What if she said no? Things would be different in second year. He'd have the guts to ask her out. No doubt about it. He drifted back to sleep, thinking about her face.

The rain lashed down, the wind blew hard, and it was pitch black, DJ stood on a muddy road, alone. Waves crashed against rocks; he couldn't see the shore. In fact, he couldn't see anything. From behind, a rush of hooves, he turned to see two shiny black horses pulling a carriage, illuminated by lights either side of a dark figure holding the reins, forcing the beasts forward at speed. DJ had no time to react, the horses were upon him, he raised his arms to his face and woke with a start, heart racing. Inside the sleeping bag was roasting. He was alone in the tent but could hear John and James talking outside. He crawled out, the sea wind blew fresh on his face.

"Sleeping beauty's awake," said John.

"More like sleeping ugly," laughed James.

DJ rubbed the sleep from his eyes. It was breakfast time. Cheese sandwiches with slices of raw onion. Washed down with milk from the boys' cows.

"I had a strange and scary dream. Woke me up."

"The boy in the bath?" John asked.

"No. Not this time. This time I was on a dirt road, rain was pelting down, I couldn't see a thing. It was dark, black really. A horse-drawn carriage rushed at me. It was like slow motion, you know, like the movies. The lights on the carriage were bright. In the driver's seat was a shadow. The horses were as black as the night, breathing hard. The shadow driver whipped them. I was caught in the light. Like... Frozen. About to be trampled and I woke up."

"Bit weird" The brothers looked at one another.

"What about you two? Any dreams?"

"Not that I remember," replied John.

"I slept like a baby. A big, beautiful baby," James grinned.

"Don't know about beautiful, but baby is just about right," ribbed DJ.

After a late breakfast they strolled the rugged shore. James took off his boots and socks and went for a paddle. DJ and John joined him. The day might have been roasting hot, but the water was winter cold. They splashed around, having a laugh. Nearby Castledawn sat silent. Watching and waiting. With frozen feet they sat on the salt-washed grass but there was no putting off the inevitable. Boots back on, they walked the field towards the old house. In the glow of the summer sun Castledawn looked anything but threatening. In fact, it looked welcoming. John brought a crowbar he found in his father's tool shed. The vestibule door was easy to pry open. For a moment, they worried that doing this could be seen as breaking and entering, but decided it was worth the risk.

The front door required a hefty push. James was first through. The hall stank.

"What the heck is that smell?" he said.

"Your feet?" laughed his brother.

"More like your breath," replied James.

"What *is* that smell? It wasn't as bad as this the last time," said DJ.

They walked to the kitchen. The sickly-sweet odour was even stronger. The smell reminded DJ of his mum's compost pit, only a lot stronger. At the cellar stairs, they heard a dull thud from above.

"What was that?" James asked.

"What?"

"That noise. What are you, deaf?"

They stood statue-still, listening. Another thud, louder – directly above them. Sounded like something being dragged across the floor.

"My God. What is that?" DJ's voice quivered. Fear rising in his chest.

"Maybe someone's upstairs. Could be looking for lead piping or something," whispered James. Remaining still, the noise stopped.

"Better have a look," said John. "Just in case."

"Eh... Maybe not," his brother was less keen.

"Aye. Could be a madman or... Well... I don't know," said DJ, braving a smile.

"Probably a rat or DJ's pigeon," said John.

"But what if it's not?" DJ asked.

John smiled, waving the crowbar in front of them, smacking it into his palm.

"Don't worry," he said. "Whoever it is, I'll introduce them to my friend."

John went to the staircase. DJ and James followed at his back. With a foot on the step and his hand on the banister. He stopped, tilted his head and listened again. There was nothing, no sound at all.

"Big rat I bet," he smiled, relieved.

Up the stairs they went, DJ and James hid behind him, you know, just in case it was a mad man. John held the crowbar like a sabre. The awful stink followed them up the stairs. They stood outside the room that DJ dreamt about. The room with the black-haired boy in the bath. The door was half opened. Church-mouse quiet they listened. No sounds came from within. John kicked the door hard and rushed in, shouting.

"Come here you blighter,"

DJ and James thought he'd seen someone or something, they stayed in the hall until they heard John laugh.

"It's alright boys. I got him."

Rushing in they saw a grinning John stood in the middle of an empty room.

"Had you going there, didn't I?" he laughed.

"Aye... Right," smiled DJ. Puffing out his chest all brave-like.

"There's nobody here," said John. "Man, nor beast."

"What about the bathroom?" James asked.

DJ's chest deflated.

"Yeah... What about the bathroom?" repeated DJ.

They edged towards the bathroom. John in front, crowbar at ready to fend off an attack. DJ and James bravely bringing up the rear. The door was closed. DJ was sure they'd left it open last time. Could've been the wind? Maybe. Without warning, John kicked at the bathroom door, running in and shouting "Come on then!" in his loudest, threatening voice. The boys ran in behind only to find it empty. Both breathed a huge sigh of relief.

"Told you it was nothing. If anyone had been here, they'd have a headache," smiled John, sitting on the edge of the tub. Smacking the crowbar into his hand.

DJ and James laughed nervously. The bathroom was neither dark nor creepy. It was just an old bathroom in a stinky old house.

"What about that." said DJ pointing to the wall opposite the tub.

It was easy to miss, but when you looked close enough, you could see the outline of a door.

"Could be just a closet," suggested John.

"Why hide it. Where's the door handle?" DJ queried.

"Wonder what's inside?" asked James.

"Let's have a look, boys."

John eased the crowbar into the small slit within the wooden wall, without much force the door popped open.

DJ and James jumped back. The three of them stood staring at an empty closet.

"Oh man. Nothing inside." said DJ disappointed and glad.

"Hold on," said John walking inside. "What's this?"

"What?" James and DJ said together.

"Look, a handle."

Before they had the chance for a closer look, John pushed and pulled at the handle until the boys saw that what had looked like bare shelves on a wall was actually a door. John opened it wide.

"Boys... It's a room."

They peered inside. The sickly stench was overpowering.

The hidden room looked like the tiniest of bedrooms. A small wooden bed was pushed up against the far wall. Light filtered through the ceiling from holes in the roof.

"Go inside," said DJ.

"Hold on now. Let me check the floor. Looks pretty rotten," John said warily.

With one foot inside, he stamped down hard. The floorboard crumbled. Totally rotten.

"Need to be careful, boys. Don't want to end up on the floor below. DJ, come here."

"What?"

"You're the lightest. You go."

"Eh… Don't think so," replied DJ. "What about James?"

"My big muscles make me heavier than you," said James.

"Aye right."

"Don't worry boy I'll hold on to you. Walk along the joists, you'll be fine."

DJ poked his head in, the stink made his throat dry and his eyes water.

"Oh, man. Do I have to?"

"Aye boy. Don't be scared."

Holding on to John, he moved inside. The floorboards creaked under his feet. It was pretty dim, the bed appeared to be the only thing in the room. He let go of John's hand.

"The joist DJ," said John. "Walk along the joist," he urged.

Almost beside the bed.

"The smell in here is terrible."

"Can you see anything?" James asked.

"Nothing. Just the bed."

"Be careful with your feet DJ."

Looked like he was walking on a tightrope. Arms horizontal. Balancing.

"I see something. Hold on."

To steady himself he grabbed at the bed. The mattress looked like rotten sack cloth stuffed with stinky straw. Maybe it was the source of the stench. His eyes adjusted to the lack of light. Above the headboard he saw black metal chains attached to the wall. He reached for one and pulled.

"Boys, there's chains here."

At the end of one chain was a small metal cuff. Too small for an adult, big enough for a child's ankle or a wrist.

"Boys. I think somebody was locked up here."

"Can you see anything else?" asked John "Wish we'd brought a bloody torch!"

"Nothing... Hold on a minute... There's something else..."

He didn't get time to finish. His right foot went through the floor.

"Wow!" DJ shouted. Steadying himself with the bed.

"DJ... I told you... Joist only," said a worried John. "You'll end up going through the floor and breaking your bloody neck," he continued, relieved that DJ hadn't been swallowed whole by the floor.

DJ pulled his foot back up and balanced himself between two floor joists.

"It's a book," he exclaimed. "There's a book," his voice, louder and excited.

"Grab it and come out! Your mum will kill us if anything happens to you," said James.

"OK. Am OK. Let me check if there's anything else."

He stuffed the dusty book into the waist band of his denims and looked around for anything else. Nothing.

Lowering his body, he peeped underneath the bed. A ceramic chamber pot sat on its own.

"Found a pee pot."

"Unless you're going to use it," grinned John. "Leave it boy. Come on."

DJ carefully inched back to John who caught his hand and dragged him out.

"The stink in there. Let's move. I need fresh air." said DJ.

"All that for a book and a chamber pot. Waste of time," said James disappointedly.

In the hall DJ pulled out the book, wiping the stoor off it with his t-shirt. He was no expert, but he knew it was old. Definitely not a paperback. There were words, he spat on his thumb, rubbing the muck off the cover. Two words. Pigmentarium Novis.

"Don't know what this means. It's not English," he said, showing it to the brothers.

"What about inside? What's it say?" asked John.

Inside the front cover it read, 'Pigmentarium Novis. *No 1 Fleshmarket Close, Edinburgh.*'

"This book is from Edinburgh," exclaimed an excited DJ. "The Fleshmarket is in the Old Town," he continued, almost shouting.

Below a door slammed shut.

"What the heck was that?" said James with fear in his voice.

The rancid smell got worse.

"Oh. Man. The smell, it's getting stronger," John said.

Another bang from downstairs.

"There's somebody down there," said James. Fear now in his stomach.

"Don't be stupid it's the wind," replied John.

Again, the sound of a slamming door. This time louder, closer.

"Somebody's there," said DJ. Heart skipping a beat.

The smell of rotten flesh overpowered their noses. DJ remembered the cow that got lost on the hill. They found it dead and bloated – it stunk so badly.

"OK boys. Time to leave. Swift like,"

They moved back into the bedroom, and John shut the door. With his ear against the wood he heard footsteps on the stairs.

Thud, thud, thud. Slow and deliberate.

"Someone's on the stairs. Quick, the window," shouted John.

Thud, thud, thud.

Footsteps, loud and dull. Not the sound of someone wearing boots. John pulled at the sash window – it was stuck fast.

Thud, thud, thud.

The footsteps were getting louder, closer.

"I'm scared," DJ said.

"Me too, boy," John replied. "But watch this."

Taking a step back he kicked at the window. Glass shattered; wood powdered. He kicked again.

Thud, thud, thud.

It was at the top of the stairs.

Thud, thud, thud.

Whoever it was. Whatever it was. Was outside the door.

John kicked the remaining shards of glass and put his head through the window, it was high but not too high. Right beneath them sat an overgrown, leafy bush.

Thud, thud, thud.

"Boys. We are going to have to jump."

Jumping was infinitely more preferable than facing whatever was making the noise.

Thud, thud, thud.

Coming inside.

James crouched on the window ledge momentarily then leaped to the ground. With the book in his waistband DJ followed his pal. Wind whistled briefly, the fresh air was momentarily soothing and then whack!

Ouch! He was slapped by hundreds of wee hands made of wood. They scraped and scratched his body.

Boomf!

He hit the ground, winded. James crawled out of the shrubbery; DJ followed him. Behind them the sound of breaking branches – John had jumped. They emerged from beneath the bush. Lying in the long grass they looked to the window. Half expecting to see something poke its head out. The sky was a beautiful pale blue and the sun shone hot. Three pairs of eyes focused on the window – whatever they were expecting didn't appear. A couple of seagulls screeched above them, breaking the silence.

"You, OK?" John asked.

"Feels like I've been dragged through a bush backwards," DJ smiled.

"Me to," said James.

They laughed hard, relieved they hadn't sustained life-threatening injuries.

Standing up, they brushed leaves and wee bits of branch from their clothes.

"Oh man. Look at my arse," said James.

The seat of his Wranglers had been totally ripped apart. His white bum cheek on show for all to see. DJ and John felt the back of their jeans and heaved a sigh of relief, both intact.

"Don't worry. Nobody will want to see your bare bum," grinned DJ.

"My mother will have a conniption when she sees this," replied James.

"Mon boys. Back to the tent. We deserve a bit of chocolate," said his brother.

They turned again and looked towards the smashed bedroom window. Nobody looked back at them.

Chapter 18

Back at the tent John set about fixing his brother's ripped jeans predicament. Ever organised, he'd packed two pairs of oilskin trousers one of which James now wore to cover his modesty. He'd sweat like mad but there was no other choice. They dined on scones and Pepsi. James waved at an Eastern Scottish tour bus full of waving and grinning tourists, probably heading to Duntulm Hotel for lunch. As the bus passed, James stood, turned and dropped his oilskins. Shaking his bum. John, mid Pepsi sip, burst out laughing. Foamy brown liquid sprayed from his nose. DJ ignored the laughing boys and was scrutinizing the book. What was it? Didn't look like any book he'd seen at school. There was a brown leather-bound bible in the shepherd's cottage when they arrived, it kind of looked like that, the cover anyway. What about the hidden room with the chains? What was it for? What was the book doing there? Many questions ran through his head, but no answers.

"Can't stop thinking about that noise," said DJ. "What the heck was it, John?"

"Dunno boy," he replied. "Maybe someone saw us and followed us?"

"Sounded awfully creepy. If it'd been a local, they'd have shouted or something? Thank God for the bush under the window. What if it had been concrete?"

"Then I don't think we would be sitting here eating scones," laughed James.

"What about this?"

DJ turned the pages of the book. They appeared unusually thick, like cardboard – yellow and water-stained. It's a miracle it'd survived given the state of Castledawn. The staining made the writing hard to read.

"You're the brain box," said John. "Read it."

"You calling me a swot?"

"Aye," said James. "We know you're the teacher's pet."

DJ was a bit of a swot, only when it came to English and History though. Maths and Arithmetic he hated. He continued flicking through the book's pages as John prepared the fire for lighting later. James was on rubbish collecting duties, making sure there was no choccy biscuit wrappers lying around waiting to be swallowed by some crofters' beast. The writing might be Latin, but he wasn't sure – the book didn't make much sense to him. Each page had handwritten notes at the sides and the top and bottom – English – like someone was taking notes. Maybe it was a schoolbook? On one page he recognized a drawing. In Edinburgh he'd stayed up late one Friday watching TV. His folks were at the next-door neighbour's party. 'Don't Watch Alone' was on STV, showing a horror movie called 'The Devil Rides Out'. Scared the heck out of him, but he couldn't stop watching it. He was sure the same symbol was drawn on a floor in the movie. Was the book something to do with the devil?

"John. Look. Have you seen anything like this before?" DJ held up the page to show him the drawing.

"Aye. It's a pentagram," he said. "We did a project about witches and black magic last Halloween. One of the girls in the class drew it. Said it was a five-pointed star used for worshipping the devil or something."

"Creepy. I think it's printed in Latin but there's English too. Looks like handwritten notes. Hard to read, the ink's faded. Book must be pretty old."

"Maybe it belonged to a witch or a wizard," said James.

"You have been watching too much TV!" smiled his brother.

"There's plenty of witches on Skye. DJ fancies a few of them," said a laughing James.

"Aye right," DJ did not look up.

There were more drawings, like what you'd see in a biology book. A heart and a brain and other organs, maybe a liver or kidney. A chapter titled Humours, underneath, four words. Sanguine. Choleric. Melancholic and Phlegmatic. Did they mean comedy, like a sense of humour? DJ had no clue. At the bottom of another page was a dagger, thin with a fancy handle – looked like the face of a ram, beneath it, more writing.

"Boys, listen," said DJ, all excited. "This part's handwritten... Bad to good. Blood for blood."

"A medical book? Maybe a First Aid book?" suggested James.

"Why would it have a pentagram?" said John.

"Good question, John. Don't know the answer."

Reading the middle pages DJ's eyes widened.

"My God. Look at this!" he exclaimed.

There was a drawing of a child, arms chained to a wall, wrists cut, blood running into an ornate goblet.

"Talk about creepy," said a nervous James. "Put it away DJ, you'll give yourself more nightmares. You'll wake crying for your mummy,"

"You more like," replied DJ.

"The chains in that room had cuffs. Maybe the family kept Monty there, you know, if he was sick. Maybe they chained him up so he couldn't infect his sisters?"

DJ's mind went into overdrive. What the heck was he looking at? What did it mean?

"Could just be a horror book DJ, or a ghost story. Who knows?" said John.

"A history book?" suggested James.

DJ was unconvinced.

"What say we go down to the castle and annoy some tourists?" said John. "Take your mind off the book."

"Aye. I could show them my bum again," laughed James. Who stood, pulled down his oilskins and shook his bum.

DJ agreed, closing the book and putting it in his bag. Couldn't stop thinking about it though.

The Eastern Scottish bus had parked close to the castle and many passengers had trekked over to the castle ruins – the boys joined them. Laughing at their funny English accents. James climbed down into the dungeon and was moaning like a ghost. An old couple looked on, laughing their heads off. Bored and ignored by the tourists, they walked to the shore. Castledawn behind them, DJ felt uneasy, like someone or something was watching them. The house looked peaceful in the heat of the late afternoon sun. Did anything evil happen there?

That night they feasted on Irish stew, drinking the last of the milk. Each held sticks salvaged from the shore and as they sat around the campfire, they poked at its orange and red embers. The sun had set, and the sky was streaked pink and purple. The Minch rippled in the breeze and there were no midges.

"Need to phone my Mum," said DJ.

"What? You want to tell her you miss her, and you love her," James mocked, kissing the air.

"Something like that."

On the road to the phone box, they sang Under the Moon of Love. There was no moon, but a few stars twinkled in the deep purple part of the sky. The three squeezed into the phone box – it smelled funny, the air inside dead and when DJ lifted the receiver, he could smell bad breath. He wanted to tell his mum about the book they found but that would cause questions from her and if she knew he'd been inside Castledawn, she'd go mental. Instead, he told her everything was fine, and he'd see her tomorrow. John called his folks with the same message.

On the way back to the tent they clowned around, walking funny and singing the theme to The Monkees. The campfire's red glow was friendly and inviting, and they had more chocolate biscuits to devour.

"Oh man, just remembered something," John said.

"What?" asked James.

"My father's crowbar, it's still in Castledawn."

"On you go. Go get it. We will wait for you here," smiled DJ.

"Eh... Don't think so," John replied. "It's bad enough going there during the day. No way I'm going at night."

"Scaredy cat," said James.

"After today? Damn right."

They sat for a couple of hours, talking and laughing and wondering what it was that chased them out of Castledawn's window. A packet of Penguins their supper. Time to hit the hay. John doused the fire and they crept into the tent and their sleeping bags.

DJ lay awake thinking about the book and who it belonged to and wondered how they could show it to folk without admitting to breaking into Castledawn. His mind drifted towards Claire. Couple of month's back he'd cycled to Uig bakers on his own and she was in there. They walked to the bridge over the River Conan and sat on the stone wall, talking and laughing for ages. Wasn't even a nice day. Pretty windy, DJ didn't mind – he'd have stayed even if it was pouring rain. He walked her to her house in Cuil and wanted to kiss her but was far too shy even though he thought she would let him. Cycling home, he kicked himself for not trying. She'd let him kiss her before, and she obviously liked him. If she didn't, why spend hours talking to him? One of these days. His mum had given him what for, being so late. Told her he'd a flat tyre and had to find someone with a pump. She looked like she didn't believe him.

***

DJ's eyes opened and he wasn't in the tent – he was in the bath at Castledawn. He tried to move, but his hand and legs were bound tight with hairy rope. His mouth was gagged by a piece of cloth. Heart thumping there were voices in the bedroom.

"He's dead. I killed him. We can't use him," said a man's voice.

"No! No. No! No!" cried a woman.

Panic shook DJ's body.

"He's dead I say. Damn you. Damn the both of us," shouted the man.

"No!" screamed the woman. "Cornelius No! Blood for blood. Bad for good. You promised."

DJ jolted awake. Breathing fast and heavy. Hot and sticky in his sleeping bag. His two pals, lay fast asleep. His breathing slowed. Outside the tent he heard wood crackle and spark, but hadn't John doused the campfire? Maybe he'd missed a spot. DJ would have to go and check, just in case a spark floated on to the tent. Wriggling free from the sleeping bag the shadow of a man moved outside. Fear crawled over him, prickling his skin as he turned to his sleeping pals, he tried to wake them. Shaking them and calling their name. Nothing. They slept. Taking a deep breath, he pulled open the tent. A man sat at the campfire. Enveloped in total darkness. Score bay had disappeared. Not one star twinkled – strange. The sky never gets dark in summer. Winter, maybe, but never summer. Standing, DJ moved hesitantly towards the man. It wasn't what he wanted to do. What he wanted was to be back in his house in Linicro. Felt like he had no say in the matter. His body, on automatic pilot, continued forward. His arm lifted; his hand reached towards the man's shoulder. With all his strength he tried to stop it, no chance, he was completely powerless. He touched the shoulder, the man turned. It was his dad!

"DJ, find him."

DJ woke up alone in the tent. Tears in his eyes. The sound of the brothers chatting outside.

Chapter 19

They left the campsite early, the brothers had to be back in time for church. They arranged a meet up in the smiddy the following day. DJ waved the boys off. Norman was in having a strupag with his mum, Catriona bounced happily on his knee.

"The explorer returns," said Norman.

"How was your trip darling?" asked his mum.

"Eh... I phoned you both nights... So, you know."

She frowned, then smiled.

"Do I get a kiss?"

"Mummy kiss. Mummy kiss," Catriona laughed.

Reluctantly, he kissed her cheek.

"That's my boy," she smiled.

"What mischief did you ruffians get up to?" asked Norman.

"Och... Nothing much. Camped. Lit a fire. Went down to the shore. That kind of thing."

"I'm sure there's more that you won't tell us," Norman probed.

"Not really, No."

Norman winked at him.

"Norman's here for you,"

"Aye boy. Came to see if you wanted to go fishing tomorrow evening? We'll take the wee dinghy out from

Kilbride. Check and see if she's still seaworthy. You interested?"

"Yes. Of course. That'll be brilliant," DJ's face lit up.

"That's grand boy. That's grand. I'll pick you up about five. We will take the Massey. Might give you a shot on the croft."

"Great. Can't wait."

DJ was doubly happy.

"Well, I'd better be off or that wife of mine will be complaining. Soon be time for church."

Norman lifted Catriona and sat her on the chair. Putting on his deerstalker hat he called out cheerio.

"Thanks Norman. For the milk," said DJ's mum.

With a wave, he was out the door.

"DJ, we need..."

"Water?"

"Yes."

"Knew it," he smiled.

After putting away his camping gear he fetched two buckets of cool, clear tobar water. The rest of the afternoon he spent playing with Catriona until five o'clock when he tuned to Radio One and the Top 40. The reception wasn't great, but anything was better than listening to a farming program on Radio Scotland!

Later, in bed, by candlelight he read the Castledawn book. Still no clue as to what it's about, but from the drawings and the handwritten notes he guessed whatever it was – it wasn't good. His eyes told him to sleep, and he stuffed the book under the mattress. Blowing out the candle, he settled under the blankets with thoughts of the fishing trip and debating whether to tell his mum about his find.

He was in the bath again. Trussed and gagged. Raised voices came from the bedroom, a man and woman argued. The bathroom door opened, a man came in, DJ closed his eyes. The man lifted him and placed him on the floor. His eyes, tight shut, DJ felt something being pulled over his head and body. The smell of tar and stoor was strong. He opened his eyes and saw he was inside a sack, shadows and light could be seen through the rough weave. The man threw him over his shoulder as if he was a sack of potatoes. In the bedroom, DJ could make out a silhouette of someone sitting, sobbing hysterically.

"Blood for blood, Cornelius. Blood for blood," she shouted, as he was carried into the hall and down the stairs.

Outside, it was windy and wet. Water seeped through the sack onto his face. He wanted to scream; the gag was tight. A deafening thunderclap sent fear through his blood vessels. Bright light flickered and penetrated the cloth. He was thrown on a hard surface, horses snorted and whinnied, the cracking of a whip. DJ's body bumped and rolled; he was in a horse-drawn carriage. Where was the man taking him? A queasiness in the pit of his stomach made him want to spew, he tried to move, but was paralysed with fear. Breathing was hard, the gag saw to that. An ear shattering thunderclap. His eyes opened. He was in his bedroom. In the safety of his house. What the heck?

***

All day DJ was excited about going fishing, on a boat! Took his mind off his horrible dream. After lunch he met up with the boys who had cut across the croft and up to their den. The hot weather had dried the bogs at the bottom of the field, making it easy to reach the smiddy fast. It was too hot and stuffy inside, so they climbed back out the window and sat in the sun; the smiddy's stone wall giving them some shade.

"Had a really bad dream last night," said DJ. "Scary. Worse than before. I was inside a sack, lying in the back of a horse drawn cart. It was pouring rain and there was thunder and lightning."

"Think your mum needs to make an appointment with Dr Samuels," grinned James. "Not sure he deals with psychos, though."

"Not funny. I'm telling you the nightmares are getting worse. So real, like."

"How come you're the only one having them?" said John. "We've all been inside Castledawn."

"DJ's weird. I keep telling you," laughed his brother.

"Aye, maybe I am."

"No 'maybe' about it," said James, still laughing.

"Oh... Forgot to say, Norman is taking me fishing on his boat. Want to come?'

John shook his head immediately.

"No thanks," he said. "I get seasick."

"Seasick? In a dinghy?"

"When? I'll come," said James.

"Later today, after his work," said DJ "We'll get you at the end of your road, round five. Norman's taking the tractor, said he'd give me a shot."

With that sorted the boys made a move; their father wanted them to finish whitewashing the byre. DJ said he'd help, but not today. He wanted to get his chores done by five. He sat for a while, watching the boys zip down the croft. Way ahead of them the Minch looked pretty calm. Not glass calm, a wind rippled the grey blue water.

His mum made mince and tatties a wee bit earlier than usual. DJ scoffed it with a big glass of milk whilst trying to feed Catriona – her mince was all over place – and he was picking bits of meat from her lap and stuffing them in her mouth. Bess got the rest. After dinner he changed into his wellies, put a jumper on, and waited for Norman. Hearing a tractor come up the road DJ said a quick cheerio to his mum and sister. Standing at the gate, he watched Norman bounce up the road on his red and white Massey Ferguson, a big smile and cheeks as red as the tractor.

"Are you right, laddie? Ready to catch some big fish? Hop on the back."

At the back of the cab, DJ climbed up behind Norman, both feet on the metal coupler used for hitching trailers.

"I asked James to come if that's OK?" he shouted over the tractor's roar.

"Och aye, boy," said Norman. "The more the merrier. We can have a wee fishing competition, eh?"

Norman opened the throttle and the tractor trundled past Miss Murchison's. As usual, she was at her door and gave them a wave. James was waiting at the end of his road and stuck out his thumb with a smile. Norman pulled up and he joined DJ at the back. On the second Totescore road they drove all the way to the end where James jumped off, opened and then closed the croft gate.

"You'll be wanting a wee shot laddie," said Norman to DJ.

"Aye. You know I do. You sure it's OK?"

"Och aye boy. We'll keep her in first though."

Norman stopped to let DJ climb into the cab. Excited, DJ sat on the red metal seat. Norman stood on the step outside the cab, issuing instructions.

"Right boy. Push down hard on the clutch. Then put her into first. Ease up on the pedal and pull the throttle with your hand. Don't worry she'll not go fast."

DJ did as he was told. His timing on the clutch and throttle wasn't perfect, but the tractor shook into life and ambled forward.

"Give it a wee bit more throttle boy," instructed Norman.

Pulling the throttle down, the tractor lurched forward, faster. Black smoke rose out of the exhaust. The field looked pretty flat, easy to navigate.

"A snail could go faster," shouted James.

Norman laughed, saying "Just ignore him DJ. You're doing grand."

DJ tried to tune out both of them and concentrate on his driving. The field wasn't as flat as it looked there were more than a few hidden bumps. The Massey's seat had no cushion, and his bum bones bashed against the metal.

"Right boy, turn left a wee bit and we will head on down this wee hill. Don't worry she's in first and she won't go any faster."

It wasn't a steep hill by any means, but to DJ it looked scary. He kept his nerve and drove to the bottom fence. He pushed his feet hard on the brake and the clutch.

Lowered the throttle, put the Massey-Ferguson into neutral and Norman yanked on the handbrake. This was something he'd practiced many times, sitting on the tractor when it was parked in Norman's shed.

"Well done, boy. Well done," said Norman patting DJ on the back. "We'll make a crofter out of you yet. From here it's Shank's pony to the shore."

Norman turned off the engine and DJ jumped out of the cab. The three of them climbed the fence towards the sea.

Kilbride was where the townships of Totescore and Linicro kept their fishing boats. A small slipway made of concrete had boulder-built walls either side. Close to the slip, Norman had constructed a wee shed and lying upturned beside it was his dark green two-seater fibreglass dinghy. Righting it, they carried it down the slipway. The tide was low as they walked to the slip's end. James stayed with the boat and DJ followed Norman to his shed. Inside was a small outboard engine, two wooden oars, and a crate full of fishing gear. DJ carried the crate and Norman, the oars and the outboard. A strong old bodach was Norman. With the outboard attached and the oars in place DJ climbed aboard and sat by James. Norman pushed the boat into the water and climbed in, sitting at the stern. With a strong arm pull of its cord, the outboard spluttered to life. A pleasant salty petrol fume hung in the air as they took to the open water. They wouldn't stray too far from shore and rounding Kilbride point, they headed towards Skudiburgh. The yellow sun reflected on the rippling water, giving it an emerald hue. The breeze was firm, but it wasn't cold. DJ loved it out on the Minch and he and James sat silent, facing forward, heading into the wind. On the other side of Kilbride was a small stone stack jutting into the air. Not as big and impressive as the Skudiburgh stack, but it was pretty cool looking. In front of the stack, locals said the water was deep even though they were close to the rocky shore. The depth meant there was a good chance of catching something big.

"Right boys," said a smiling Norman turning off the outboard. "We'll give it a go here. This is my lucky spot."

The dinghy bobbed as they readied their lines. Each held a square wooden frame with fine orange twine wrapped around, ending with three hooks, bright coloured lures and a small lead weight. Norman threw his line port-side, the boys, starboard. All hoping to be first to catch a bite.

"You know DJ," said Norman. "I was thinking you could speak to Constable Williams in Uig about the history of Castledawn. Don't know why I didn't think of him before. He's a bit of a local history buff. Loves all things old and is very knowledgeable about the North End. Ask him about the house and its owners."

DJ, about to say thanks was cut off by James shouting, "Wow! I've got a bite... maybe two!"

"Reel it in boy. Reel it in," encouraged Norman.

James wrapped the line round the frame quick as, then placed it on the deck using his foot to hold it steady, the remaining line he pulled with his hands and out of the water popped two decent sized mackerel. Landing both fish Norman helped by unhooking them and knocking their heads with a wooden mallet until they stopped jumping and squirming. James was casting his line when DJ got a bite. A big one. Excited, he pulled and pulled and up came three mackerel. Wow! The fish jerked something fierce, he was surprised how strong they were, but he managed to reel them in. Once unhooked, Norman stunned all three fish into submission. So pleased was DJ and glad he'd caught more than James – the competition was definitely on. Norman landed three mackerel too, and for a good hour they fished the same spot. Not every catch was mackerel. There were some small red and brown fish, like the ones at Uig Pier – those got tossed back. It took less than two hours for them to catch over twenty fish.

"Well shipmates. We've had a good haul. What say we head for shore?" said Norman.

"Aye aye, Captain," laughed both boys.

Norman fired up the outboard and headed back to Kilbride. The sun had shrunk as it crept towards Uist, preparing to sink below the horizon. The tide was high at the slip, DJ volunteered to get his wellies wet. He jumped over the side, splashing into the water and pulling hard on the bow rope. Norman and James decanted and they all dragged the boat to the shed, where the boys threw their fish haul into a plastic bucket. From the shed Norman produced a wooden slab and a gutting knife. Above them, black and grey seagulls spotted there was a chance of some grub – they screeched and squawked in delight. The boys watched as Norman gutted the fish with ease. The stainless-steel knife was sharp as anything. He placed the fish on the slab, slicing the heads clean off before running the blade down the inside of the belly and removing the guts. The end result was beautiful fish fillets. After cleaning the wood with Minch water, he wiped the knife clean with a rag. Once everything was locked away, DJ and James carried the bucket of filleted fish to the tractor. Norman said he'd give the fish a good clean at his house and deliver them in the morning. They'd caught twenty-two mackerel. Funny thing though, both DJ and James were not keen on fish – only eating when forced by their parents. The drive to Linicro was slow and after dropping James off, DJ was delivered to his gate.

"Thanks Norman," said DJ. "I had a brilliant time. And thanks for the info about Constable Williams."

"Glad you enjoyed it son. Glad you enjoyed it. Tell your mum I'll drop the fish off tomorrow."

With a wave and a red-faced smile, Norman took off. DJ went into the house happy and absolutely famished. His mum made him toast and cheese and a cup of sweet cocoa. He told her about the fishing, and she was glad he'd had a good time. Catriona was fast asleep, DJ and his mum stayed up late listening to the radio and he was so tempted to tell her about the book but resisted the urge to do so.

"DJ, DJ. Wake up. DJ..."

DJ woke to his dad's voice.

"DJ, DJ are you awake?"

The voice came from outside. Getting out of bed, he opened the skylight and stuck his head out, his dad stood at the gate.

"DJ, you need to find him son. He needs your help."

"Who dad? Who?"

"He needs your help, son. Find him. He's in the water. He's cold and he wants to go home."

His dad waved and smiled. DJ tried to tell him to wait, that he'd come downstairs. He woke up. Looking at skylight window, the window was closed. It was still summer dark, and he reckoned he'd only been asleep for a short time. What did his dad mean? Was he talking about the black-haired boy in the bath? He needed help. Was in water and wanted to go home. What did it mean? Unable to get back to sleep, he replayed everything that had happened recently. It all began the day they entered Castledawn. The dreams, his dad. Everything. Castledawn was where the answers were, but what was the question, and where was the black-haired boy?

Chapter 20

Each night DJ's dream was the same. His dad called his name from the gate and every time he attempted to go downstairs, something stopped him and he woke up. Every night he read from the Pigmentarium Novis, and was still no closer to understanding what the words meant. The temptation to tell his mum was ever present – especially about the dreams, but worried if he told her about seeing his dad, it would upset her. The past six months she'd been the happiest he'd seen her in a long time, and he didn't want to ruin it by talking about seeing and hearing her dead husband. He hadn't seen much of the boys as they were busy doing the hay with their father. DJ helped when they did the baling, but his mum was working extra shifts to cover holidays, so most of the week he spent babysitting Catriona. Didn't mind it too much, and it gave him time to think and to read.

Friday afternoon DJ took Catriona to see Miss Murchison. The old girl was very fond of her, and Catriona liked to visit because she got a chocolate biscuit or two. DJ didn't mind visiting either. He knew she was lonely with only her dog for company, and she had always been good to him. What with the odd jobs and paying decent money. He was five pounds away from the eighty he needed to order his dream bike: a bronze-coloured Raleigh Chopper GT Sprint – advertised in Maggie's

Great Universal catalogue as 'flamboyant tangerine.' It was on Bruntsfield Place a couple of years ago he first saw one and had dreamed about it ever since. The Sprint wasn't as popular as the regular Chopper, he liked that, it meant not many people had it and with its racing handlebars it looked totally cool.

Miss Murchison was sitting reading the People's Friend when DJ knocked.

"Miss Murchison it's DJ and Catriona."

"Oh, come away in son. Come away in."

Catriona ran to her, giving her a hug. The old woman spoke to her in Gaelic. M'eudail and a thasgaidh. DJ knew it meant something like my darling or my dear – she said it every time she saw his sister.

"How have you been?" asked DJ.

"Can't complain son. Can't complain. All the better for seeing this wee one."

"She wanted to see you. Didn't you Catriona? You wanted to visit with Miss Murchison?"

"Mmm hmm," nodded Catriona who was playing with the buttons on the old lady's cardigan.

"And how's your mum? Portree Hospital working her hard?"

"Oh, aye. All this week she's worked. Somebody's on holiday I think."

"Oh, that's nice son. That's nice."

"And you are OK yourself?"

"Aye, well I'm grand. Just grand. Oh... Here... I've got a wee job for you. There's five pounds in it. Are you interested?"

"Aye... Sure," he replied with excitement "That's all I need to buy my new bike. What needs done?"

"Alistair from Totescore delivered a load of peat, and it needs stacking beside the coal. Only take you an hour or so. I'll look after the wee one."

"Sure. No problem."

He was happy to get out in the sun and leave Catriona with someone else for a while. The wooden wheelbarrow he found by the shed was just the ticket for the job – it'd seen better days though. Only part that wasn't worn was the cast iron wheel; all the wood was dotted with woodworm holes. He got to work filling the barrow, transporting the peat and stacking it neatly by the coal stack. Two things occupied his mind – the new bike and Castledawn. The answer to all the weirdness was there – he was sure of it, and he knew they'd have to take one last trip to Score. Would have to wait, though, next week was the Linicro sheep shearing fank. The peat stacking only took an hour to complete and Miss Murchison handed him his five-pound note.

"You're a good boy DJ. Really. I'd be lost without you. And as for this wee darling," the old girl tickled Catriona's belly making her squirm and giggle. Oh, and by the way son, I remembered something about Castledawn. Thought you'd like to know, since you have taken a keen interest in the place. Monty, the boy, he passed away in his parents' bathroom, the one upstairs. They found the wee soul lying in the tub – no water in it, mind you. That bathroom was always cold for some reason and if he had an asthma attack, that's where he'd go. The cool air you see. Helped with his breathing. Was his mother that found him. She never got over that. Never."

"Wow! Very interesting. Thanks Miss Murchison."

DJ sang Summer Nights from the movie Grease to Catriona on the way home – she loved it. Especially the chorus when he shouted.

"A wella, wella, wella, well."

Catriona thought this the funniest thing ever.

When his mum arrived, the first thing he did was present her with the five-pound note.

"Mum, I've done it. I've got enough for the bike. Can you call Maggie to order it? Now? Please."

"Give me a minute darling,"

"The sooner it's ordered the quicker I'll get... Please mum?'

"OK, OK... OK!" she smiled. "Can I get changed first?"

Standing by the phone, DJ could barely contain himself, holding on to his mum's arm as she spoke to Maggie.

"Hi Maggie, it's me. How are you? Great. We are all fine. Well, except I have one very excited teenager hanging on to me. DJ's finally saved enough money for the bike I told you about. Can you order it, please? That's right the Raleigh Chopper Sprint. The bronze one. Tangerine, is it?'

She looked at DJ. He nodded his head. The bronze colour was also called tangerine.

"He's nodding furiously, so yes. The flamboyant tangerine. Oh, thanks Maggie. DJ is about to explode. Yes, I'll tell him. See you soon. Bye-bye now."

She hung up, DJ stared.

"So?"

"So, what?" she teased.

"Mum... How long will it take to get here?"

"Well... You know we are not living in Edinburgh."
"Mummm!" he pleaded.
"She'll phone the order in. Reckons it'll take a week or so."
"That long?"
"Sorry darling, it's got to come all the way from Manchester. I'll visit Maggie tomorrow, pay for it. What do you have planned?"
"Tomorrow?"
"Yes, DJ. Tomorrow."
"Mum, it's the fank. I told you."
'Oh right. OK. Patience son, soon you'll have a beautiful tangerine bike."
"Bronze." he smiled.

***

In bed, he flicked through the Pigmentarium Novis. Still didn't give up much information, but he kept going back to one drawing in particular. It was that of an adult and a child. Handwritten under it was,
'Bad to good, needs blood for blood.'
'Blood for blood' was written on a lot of pages. Chanting in his head. 'Blood for blood' – it's what the woman in his dream screamed. 'Blood for blood'.
"DJ... DJ... Are you awake?"
DJ's eyes opened.
"DJ... DJ, son..."
He knew he was dreaming, but he so wanted it to be real. Wanted to go downstairs -, and out the door, into his dad's arms, but. he was compelled to go to the skylight. Outside, at the gate, his dad waited.

"DJ, you have to find him. He wants to go home. He's cold, DJ. Help him."

DJ tried to call out, no sound came from his mouth. 'Find him.'

DJ woke up. It was light, but no noise came from downstairs, must be early. He'd stay awake until he heard his mum getting up. Today was fank day!

Chapter 21

After porridge DJ heard the rumbling of a tractor coming down the road. He knew it was the boys and their father. He was ready to go.

"Don't forget your lunch, darling," said his mum, pointing to a Tupperware box.

She walked out with him. The grey Ferguson appeared with the boys sitting in the trailer. Murdo, their father, waved to DJ's mum shouting "Good Morning Annie. Lovely day for shearing sheep."

"Be good," said his mum.

DJ climbed into the trailer, Murdo opened up the throttle and the tractor lurched forward.

"Guess what?" DJ shouted as they bounced down the road.

"What?" said John.

"Come on... Guess?'

"You asked Miss Murchison out on a date?" smiled James.

"Funny... Come on... Guess?"

"We give up... What?"

"I ordered the bike! Got a fiver from James's girlfriend... I mean Miss Murchison yesterday. Mum ordered it from Maggie's catalogue."

"Really? The Sprint?"

"Aye... Should be here next week."

"Brilliant," said John.

The wee tractor turned off at the pens, from there it was a rocky ride to the fank – pretty painful on the old bum. Inside, the fank was a hive of activity, the air alive to the sound of hundreds of sheep baahing. For the past two days, from way up behind the Linicro rocks, the shepherd had brought the township's sheep down from the hill and enclosed them in a grassy fenced off field which led to a couple of stone-walled pens. Each pen was stuffed full of hairy four-legged beasts separated by a rusting iron gate. The sheep in the front pen were dragged through a rickety grey wooden gate and handed to a crofter with clippers in his hand. As the front pen emptied, sheep herded in from the back pen and as that emptied so more sheep were driven in from the grassy field. A sheep shearing conveyor belt of beasts in constant motion.

The three of them climbed the dry-stone wall and stood amongst a group of chattering crofters. The brothers' father joined them, and they picked out a spot where he'd do the shearing. It wasn't all men. Ina and Marie were sisters who lived on the croft next to the Post Office. Known as the township spinster sisters, they wore green wellies and blue flowery pinnies. Wearing the same headscarf, both ladies had bright red cheeks, calloused hands and big smiles. They wouldn't shear, their job was collecting and rolling the freshly shorn fleeces. From a rust red rectangular metal frame hung a long brown sack that flapped around in the wind. This would be stuffed full of fleeces once the shearing began. The ladies had fashioned a makeshift table from two wooden doors sitting on top of a couple of rusty brown oil drums. Here they'd spread the fleeces and roll them ready for the big sack. DJ and James knew they'd be inside the sack. Packing down the fleeces with their feet and catching ones thrown in by Ina and Marie. It was a dirty, smelly job, but DJ loved it.

With each crofter at their preferred spot, the annual sheep shearing fank began. John's job was to haul sheep from the pen and hand them off to a shearer – not an easy job. You needed to be strong. DJ and James would help the crofters hold down the sheep whilst they clipped away at the woolly fleece with metal hand clippers. Once the fleece was off, they'd load the sheep dose gun with thick yellow deworming liquid, stick the nozzle into the side of the animal's mouth, and pull the trigger – a shot of liquid went down its gullet. After dosing they'd mark the sheep with red paint, signifying they belonged to Linicro Township. From a huge pot of thick, stinky paint the boys used a stick to mark the left side of the shorn sheep with two lines. Once marked, they'd set them free to run to the middle of the fank, which was covered in luscious green grass. DJ and James absolutely loved dosing and marking. Gave them a real sense of satisfaction. It was also a good laugh as they would chase each other about with the red stick and try to mark each other's jeans. DJ would also fire a glob of sheep dose at James, rarely did it hit, though.

By lunchtime, they were ravenous. Murdo had brought a Thermos flask filled with sweet, milky tea and they enjoyed their cheese scones being washed down with the hot liquid. After lunch the bodachs chatted in Gaelic, laughing and smoking roll-ups.. DJ stretched out on a patch of grass and gazed up to the sky. High above soared a golden eagle, it didn't look that big to DJ, but John told him an eagle could lift a small lamb with its razor-sharp talons.

Break over, it was time for DJ and James to get into the fleece sack and start packing the wool. Climbing on the table, they pulled themselves up and into the scratchy sack. Inside it stank – a mixture of sheep dung, grass and oil – it was roasting too. Ina and Marie began throwing in the rolled fleeces. James grabbed them, pushed them down and both boys stamped down hard, packing them tight. They had to watch out for ticks on the fleeces, making sure they didn't transfer to them. James had one on his head the year before, sucking at his blood, DJ didn't want the same. As the sack filled their heads popped out the top and they waved to everyone. The old crofters ignored them, but the sisters laughed. When full, the sack was lowered and a new one hoisted. With a big needle and thick twine, the sisters sowed the sacks shut.

The fank lasted three days. God knows how many sheep got sheared, but to DJ it seemed like millions. Each evening they'd travel home on Murdo's tractor, dog-tired but happy. First thing his mum made him do was to wash – he stank, Catriona made a show of holding her nose every night. His mum checked for ticks – none were found. He was so tired he dropped off to sleep without reading and every night his dad woke him up. Got so that he looked forward to dreaming. It wasn't scary and he got to see his dad smile.

The black-haired boy was cold and wanted to go home.

Chapter 22

DJ could hardly breathe, his heart pumped fast, and he'd the biggest smile on his face. Doing his chores, he could barely contain his excitement. Today was the day. The day Great Universal would deliver his bike. Could be anytime. By mid-afternoon there was still no sign of it... John and James had joined him in the smiddy, and they waited, and waited, for the delivery van to arrive.

"This Saturday let's go to Score; I want my crowbar back." said John.

The radio played David 'Hutch' Soul, singing Silver Lady. DJ wondered if Starsky could sing.

"I can take my new bike," smiled DJ, singing the Silver Lady chorus.

He was looking forward to taking the Chopper Sprint on its maiden voyage – but he wasn't looking forward to going back to Castledawn. Not after the last time. Whatever it was that chased them last time, was waiting.

Finally, the rumble of a diesel engine and a blast from a horn got them out of the smiddy door, it was a tight squeeze. A Great Universal Transit parked in front of the house. The driver was talking to DJ's Mum. Nervous and happy DJ stood at the back door with the boys as the driver jumped in and pulled out a large brown box covered in plastic. His mum signed a paper on a clipboard, the delivery guy jumped back in the van, made a three-point turn and drove off. The three of them tore at the box like cartoon Tasmanian Devils. Catriona and his mum looked on as the bike was revealed. Wow! It looked even better than it did in the catalogue. It was more orange than bronze, Day-Glo, almost, but it didn't bother DJ. With a three-speed gear and racing handlebars – the bike was a total cracker. Each of them took turns, having a shot, and they played with it well into the evening. After the brothers left for home, DJ put his shiny new bike in the back shed. It had no lock on the door, but this wasn't Edinburgh. Nobody would steal it.

***

When Saturday came, the hot weather had well and truly disappeared. The sky was dark and cold. A thick mist rolled down from the hill and the Linicro rocks were nowhere to be seen. John had phoned, he and James had to go to Portree with their mother to get kitted out for school – new clothes, shoes and exercise books. They wouldn't head down to Score until late afternoon. DJ hoped the weather would clear up by then. The boys showed up at four. John with his trailer and James with a shoulder bag. Both had had haircuts.

"Nice haircut," said DJ. "Just wait a minute and I'll get the red paint to mark your side," he laughed.

"At least our mother doesn't give us a bowl cut," said James, grinning big at his joke.

"Right boy, are you ready?" said John.

"Aye. I think so. Not sure about Castledawn though."

"I know boy. I know. This will be the last time. Promise," said John with a reassuring smile.

The camping gear in the bike trailer was covered with a piece of tarpaulin. The weather hadn't cleared, and it looked like more rain was coming from Waternish.

"Let's get going. Get ahead of these showers," said John.

DJ wheeled out his Sprint pride and joy and they took off for Score Bay.

They didn't make it out of Linicro before the rain arrived in driving sheets. They wore oilskin jackets of bright orange – at least the wind was at their back, helping them push through Kilmuir. The rain didn't stop. By the time they reached Score it was absolutely pelting it down, being so close to the shore meant that they got battered by a salty wind. Pitching a tent when it's bucketing down wasn't easy, but John managed pretty well. DJ and James helped with the ground sheet and the rain cover. By the time it was pitched the rain was driving sideways and it was pretty misty. Duntulm Castle had disappeared, concealed by the grey. The shadow of Castledawn was visible, just. Standing on the road looking in the direction of Score's cliffs, DJ saw nothing, other than low-hanging clouds. It was like someone had dropped an atomic bomb and the world had ended. No survivors except three teenage boys in a tent on Skye.

"So," said John. "Are we going or what?"

They'd sat in the tent for an hour, hoping the rain would stop. It didn't. It was worse. A wind blustered across the Minch, turning the rain into millions of water bullets aimed at everyone and everything.

"What? You still want to go?" asked James.

"Aye. Want my crowbar back. Maybe we can try to get into the cellar."

"Em... I don't know about that," said DJ. "What if what we heard last time lives in the cellar?"

"Told you before, old houses make noises."

"Aye, but what we heard was someone walking. You were there you heard it too."

"Don't worry boy," said John with a smile. "Once I get my crowbar nothing will harm us."

DJ and James weren't convinced. No way was it wind blowing through an old house. No way at all. Did the wind walk up the stairs and go into the bedroom? Doubt it. Scared, they put their trust in John. He was older, bigger and tougher, and if anyone or anything attacked them, DJ and James could at least hide behind him.

Visibility was almost zero. Castledawn had disappeared in the haar. Zipping up their oilskins, they made for the shore, which couldn't be seen but waves could be heard crashing onto the rocks. The boys followed the fence along the shoreline till they stood in front of the house. They stuck close together, moving like one wide-bodied person. Hard rain bounced off their faces and found its way in through their oilskins, running down their necks. Standing, staring, DJ and James would've preferred to keep on walking, but John was determined, and he wasn't scared or at least, he didn't show that he was scared. The sky looked like it had dropped to earth and there was no sign of summer as they walked towards Castledawn's vestibule door.

The door was shut tight. Strange. The last time they'd jemmied it open with the crowbar. John reached to turn the doorknob. He twisted and pushed. Nothing. The door wouldn't budge it was, as if someone had locked it with a key.

"What?" asked DJ, puzzled. He was now thinking he'd rather be inside the house, out of the rain.

"The door won't open," replied John. "Feels like it's locked."

"But we busted it open the last time. Some of the wood from the frame fell on the ground, I remember," said James.

"You think someone fixed it?" asked DJ.

"Aye, but who?"

"We could go back to the tent. Wait for the rain to stop. Maybe get a fire going," said James hopefully.

"Good idea," seconded DJ.

"We're here now, boys," said John ignoring them "Looks like we are going in through the window."

DJ and James followed John to the broken vestibule window, and they crawled through. Outside the heavy black front door, they stood. Fear showed on DJ's face, James's too. With his hand on the doorknob and his shoulder to the door John turned the knob and gave a big push. The door scraped open and immediately they were hit by the sickly-sweet rotten smell, worse than before. Acrid and penetrating. DJ felt sick. Water streamed down both walls in the hall and the floor was one massive puddle. It was dark, dank and bloody creepy.

"Torch," said John.

Nobody answered.

"Who brought the torch?"

Still no answer.

"Oh, for God's sake, don't tell me nobody brought a torch."

"Thought you had it," said James to his brother.

"I thought James had it," winced DJ.

"Well... Looks like we are going in without a light."

DJ and James were far from feeling happy and they stuck like glue to John. Without summer sunlight the place resembled something out of a Hammer horror film and DJ had watched enough of them to know what happened when you break into a creepy old house.

They moved as one through the flooded hall.

"Nothing to be frightened of boys," said John. "It's just a house."

Reaching the bottom of the stairs, DJ looked over towards the kitchen and saw it was cloaked in darkness. He could just about make out the creepy corner and the shadow of the arch where the cellar steps hid. No way was he going down there today. Absolutely no way.

A stream of fetid grey water flowed down the stairs. Rain poured in from every hole in the roof. John was first on the stair. Looked like he was walking through a river. DJ and James stuck behind him. Ascending, the putrid smell brought tears to their eyes. James gagged a few times. Outside a raging wind blasted against the walls and windows. They stopped at the top. The upstairs hall was wet and dark, the floor, squelchy underfoot and the *smell*! Sulphur, decomposition and sweetness. DJ could have barfed. As one they moved towards the master bedroom. The door was closed. Last time it was open – DJ was positive he saw it flap open just before he dived out the window.

"I'm not going in. I'll wait here," DJ said.

"Aye. Me too." murmured James.

John pushed at the door. It opened easily and, like everywhere else, the bedroom was dark and stinky. Heavy water dripped from the ceiling. John grabbed his brother's arm and dragged him through the door.

"You are coming with me... Just in case."

They crept towards the broken window scanning the floor for the crowbar. The haar had begun to creep inside.

"Eyes open boy. Check the... What was that?"

A loud *thunk* came from the bottom of the stairs. Loud but dull. DJ's heart jumped, almost stopped as he sidled towards the room.

Thwack!

The door slammed shut in his face. He nearly had a heart attack.

His hand twisted and turned the knob and he pushed at the door. It was locked. He banged on the wood with balled fists.

"Boys... Boys... The door... It's locked!" he screamed.

Foowump!

The noise from the stair.

Foowump!

Something was coming up.

DJ banged and banged with all his strength, he could hear the boys fiddling and pulling the door from the other side. It wouldn't open.

Foowump!

Foowump!

It was getting closer. Whatever it was.

"Boys... Boys... Something's coming up the stairs. Let me in." DJ panicked.

Foowump!

Foowump!

At the top of the stairs.

DJ beat on the door with all his might. John and James were shouting and pulling on the doorknob.

Thud!

DJ saw a shadow. Somebody was there.

"Boys... It's here... it's..."

The thing closed in on him. It was coming for DJ.

"Boys... Boys... Get out. Get out..." Water streamed down the bedroom door – black blood from the building's veins. DJ was in full fight or flight mode. Flight was his choice, but his feet were stuck to the ground, no movement. After a panicky struggle he unglued himself and fled towards the door opposite. It was shut tight, and his hands slipped and fumbled on the wet, cold doorknob. He managed to pry it open just enough to slip through, but before he could escape, the nightmare materialized before him. Out of the shadows a mass of worms, bloodworms, in the shape of person. What the heck! Squirming and snapping black teeth. Too red. There were eyes but no face. As it lunged towards him DJ forced his way through the part-open door. Glancing back, he locked eyes with the beast for a second – a nano second – before spinning round and slamming the door shut behind him, his feet felt like they were sinking. Stuck in a quagmire, before he could scream, the floor swallowed him like quicksand.

Chapter 23

"DJ, DJ. Son, wake up. DJ, DJ. Wake up. He's close son. Find him."

DJ's eyes opened, he was lying, staring up at the hole in the ceiling where he'd fallen through. His back hurt, so did his head and his brain felt fuzzy. Where the heck? It was dark -too dark – fear gripped his chest, tight. The kitchen, I'm in the kitchen. The kitchen where stairs lead to the cellar. Flight mode engaged. He could move. He was OK. Nothing broken at least. From the staircase, he heard.

Foowump.

Foowump.

That noise again. That thing. The bloodworm beast.

He was on his feet and running through the hall like he was doing the 100-metre dash. Waterfall walls and loch floor, he moved so fast he was almost aquaplaning. The door at the end of the hall was shut. Please don't be locked, please don't be locked. Please let me out of here. Grabbing the door knob he pulled with all his might – thankfully it gave no resistance – he flew into the vestibule. Scrambling like mad he made it out of the window, with no looking back. If the bloodworm beast was behind him, he didn't want to see it. Not now. Not ever. He flopped into a pool of water beneath the window. The sky was darker than before and the rain heavier. The wind, gusting. How long had he been lying inside? Not long. Running round the back of the house he found the bush beneath the bedroom window, he searched for the boys. No sign of them, his hope of seeing them laughing and crawling from underneath, dashed.

"John! James!" he screamed into the wind.

He circled the house.

"John! James!" at the top of his lungs.

Nothing.

The rain drilled into him; the salt wind howled. Maybe they'd gone back to the tent. Maybe they were looking for him. From within the grey, he found the mud track that led to the road. Visibility was poor, he could hardly see anything in front of him, the wind pushed him towards the road, but the ground was heavy going, thick mud sucked at his feet, it took all his strength to move. Where was the road? A fence appeared from within the haar. He was close. Climbing across the wire, he landed on springy grass. Black asphalt appeared under his feet. Thank God. He walked towards the campsite. In the distance, something moved. Through the mist he saw an outline of something big – strange he couldn't hear the rumble of an engine. It was horses and they were almost upon him, their metal shoes sparked on the road. Two bright lights shone either side of a silhouette. Two eyes searching in the haar. What the…? It was the horse-drawn carriage from his dream. Panic once again engulfed him; he turned and ran. Where to go? Where to hide? His mind and his feet raced. It was downhill. Towards Duntulm castle. He could jump the fence again, but that'd take him back to Castledawn, and that was the last place he wanted to go. He stayed on the road, the wind swiping at him, salt in his mouth and stinging his eyes. Horses and wheels rattling behind him. Closer.

He ran for his life.

Mr. Mackenzie, the Coastguard! DJ's lungs and brain worked overtime. Heart bursting in his chest. The fear kept him moving. Turning he saw how close the carriage was. The creepy lights illuminating an even creepier figure sat at the reins. Two silver-black shadows in front of it. Heads bobbing, breathing hot and hard, the sound of hooves getting louder, getting closer. He wished he'd worn his Golas instead of wellies. Rounding the corner past the castle, he thought about crossing the field and hiding in the dungeon, but what if the horses followed? Smashing through the gate running on the soft grass. Where would he go? He'd end up at the edge of the steep cliff with only the sea and rocks below to break his fall. The road was his only option. The Coastguard's house his destination. The wind, now at his back, pushed him, willing him forward. The rain rattled off his oilskin. Uphill now, adrenaline coursing through his body and he kept on. Ahead, a dark cross at the side of the road. The Coastguard sign. He was close, but so were the horses and the carriage with their creepy lights and whoever was at the reins. He zoomed past the sign, all downhill to the Coastguard's and safety. The adrenaline surge was receding. His legs wobbled, sweat ran down his back. His poor heart, beating ten to the dozen. The horses were gaining, louder and louder. He could see the house in the shadows – the Land Rover parked outside. Mr. Mackenzie was in, thank God. Nearly there boy. Nearly, but it wasn't enough. The black horses were on him. Caught in the carriage lights, he saw the face of his pursuer. From under a black top hat, he saw him. Dead eyes black and skin of grey and the horses about to pummel him. DJ dived to the side of the road and rolled down a hillock. The horses followed, the lights and the man and his dead eyes staring. Back on his feet, DJ ran... *Whoosh*... Frigid water. DJ sank into the lochan in front of the Coastguard's house. Darkness absorbed him. Eyes wide open, his arms above him as he descended into the peaty deep. A thought crossed his mind, he'd always wondered how deep this lochan was – now he'd find out.

Someone grabbed his hand; his feet touched the muddy bed. The lochan wasn't that deep after all, and Mr. Mackenzie had come to save him. DJ's head broke the surface his lungs filled with air and holding his hand was his dad. The fear and cold evaporated. A loving heat radiated from his dad's hand, instantly warming DJ's body. Waist deep in the lochan DJ felt at total peace. A gentle pull brought him to the grassy bank.

"You did it, son. You found him."

DJ tried to crawl from the water on to the grass, wanting desperately to hug his dad so tight but he was no longer there. DJ was alone and bone cold, and to make matters worse his left leg was caught on something beneath the surface of the lochan. The rain stopped, he looked to the hillock, no sign of the horses. No lights. No dead eyed driver. Nothing. Just him with one leg stuck. He tried to sit up on the bank, pulling his leg as hard as anything, but couldn't get purchase on the greasy grass. No choice. He lowered himself back into the peat stained cold, the water at his neck and his searching hand found something wrapped around his foot – a metal chain! Twisting and shaking and pulling, he freed his foot. Still in his hand he yanked the chain. It gave a wee bit but felt as if it was attached to something. He scrambled up the lochans bank and managed to get himself standing. The haar was lifting, and his welly boots were brim-full of water. No wonder he could hardly move. The chain remained in his hand; it looked old; he pulled it harder; it was dragging something... Maybe it was a boat anchor? One bigger heave unstuck it and knocked him off balance onto his bum. The water drained from his wellies, his hands felt like blocks of ice, but he continued pulling the chain – whatever was on the end was close to breaching the surface. He stood up again, feet squelchy and frozen and he pulled and pulled, walking further from the water's edge. A final tug brought whatever it was out of the water; it wasn't an anchor – the chain was wrapped around a black sack.

Looking at the bundle's shape, DJ realised what he had found.

Chapter 24

With the haar receding and the wind calming, DJ saw a plume of smoke rising from the Coastguard's chimney. A light shone warm and friendly, and he thought how great it would be to sit in front of the fire and warm his freezing hands. He knocked on Mr Mackenzie's kitchen door. The hard wood stung his knuckles. The outside light came on and he heard footsteps, then the click of a lock. The door opened revealing the friendly face of the Duntulm Coastguard.

"Oh, here DJ what happened to you, boy?" said a worried Mr Mackenzie. "Come away in."

"Hi Mr Mackenzie. I'm OK. A wee bit wet. A big bit cold but am OK."

"Come in, son. Let's get you in front of the fire."

"That would be great, but we need to go to our camp. I need to check on John and James. We got lost in the mist. I need to find them. Will you help me, please? I'll tell you all about it."

"Right boy. OK. Let me get you a wee blanket at least and I'll put my boots on."

He reappeared with a tartan Skye woollen mill blanket and wrapped it round DJ's shoulders, DJ pulled it tight to his body. Underneath the scratchy wool he shivered.

"Oh, you're shaking laddie. We need to get you warmed up."

"Aye am freezing but can we check on my pals first please?"

Mr Mackenzie grabbed his jacket and his Coastguard hat, and they got into the Land Rover. The rain clouds separated, and a hint of purple summer night sky peeped through as they drove towards the campsite.

"What time is it?" DJ asked.

"Just after nine, laddie. What a day it's been, eh?"

"You can say that again," DJ replied, shivering like a jelly.

"What on earth happened DJ? How did you get so wet?"

"I fell in to your lochan. Didn't see it because of the mist."

"Eh?' said the Coastguard. Confusion in his face.

"Aye... Eh indeed," DJ gave him a smile.

The haar lifted completely, Castledawn sat quiet and benign. Fear twisted in DJ's gut. Then he saw the two brothers standing outside the tent. Thank God they're OK. Mr Mackenzie stopped, rolled down the window and shouted them over. DJ had the scratchy blanket over his head and was smiling underneath it.

"Alright boys?" he said.

Mr Mackenzie told the boys to hop in the back. He reversed down the road till he came to the castle's parking area. Turning the Land Rover, he took off towards his house.

"DJ boy. Oh DJ!" said a relieved John. "We're so glad to see you. We thought you got lost and drowned or something."

"Aye... We were scared about what your mum would do to us for losing her darling DJ," smiled James, patting DJ's back.

"What happened?" asked John.

"Aye DJ. What happened?" repeated Mr Mackenzie.

"If you get me some dry clothes and a mug of tea, I'll tell you."

"That we can do, boy. That we can do. I'll need to phone your parents."

DJ wanted to talk to his mum but was only thinking about the heat from Mr Mackenzie's fire.

At the house, Mr Mackenzie gave DJ a change of clothes, his son Ian's gear might've been too big, but they were dry and warm. The three boys warmed their hands and feet in front of the living room fire. Mr Mackenzie made them mugs of tea.

"I've got some biscuits, too. Don't know where the wife has put them. You drink up and get yourself toasty. I'll call your folks, tell them you're OK. Lucky, I put the fire on. It was such miserable day and with the wife visiting the boys in Glasgow I wanted to make myself cosy like," he smiled.

Sipping their tea. James was first to speak.

"What the heck happened DJ? We were so scared. We thought we'd find you outside. We nearly broke our necks jumping out that window again."

"At least I found my crowbar," smiled John.

"Seriously, we were so worried and it's not because we like you – we didn't want to explain to your mum that we lost you!" said James with a cheeky grin.

Mr Mackenzie returned.

"Right lads. DJ, that's your mum on the phone. John, I spoke to your father. Told him I'll be bringing you home tonight. Didn't tell him much just said the rain waterlogged your tent."

"Good man. Thank you, Mr Mackenzie."

DJ spoke to his mum assuring her he was OK and that with the weather being so bad, they had asked Mr Mackenzie's help. His mum sounded worried but was glad to hear everyone was safe. She said she nearly had conniptions when she heard the Coastguard's voice on the phone. Her mind raced, worried something terrible had happened. DJ repeated they were all fine and they'd just got soaking wet. Once they got dry, Mr Mackenzie would give them a lift home. The rest of the story he'd tell her face to face.

Back in front of the fire, DJ was the first to talk, and it wasn't about Castledawn.

"We need to go to lochan," he said in serious tone. "I pulled something from it."

"Lochan? What were you doing there?" asked James.

"Well... Don't laugh... I fell in looking for Mr Mackenzie's front door. I couldn't see a thing in the mist."

"Eh?" said John, confused.

"Aye. Walked right into it. It's not deep. My foot got stuck on something. A chain under the water and when I pulled it, I found a bundle attached to it..."

"A what?" said John?

"Something wrapped in a sack."

"Well, if you're up to it, we can have a wee look now," said Mr Mackenzie. "I'll get my torch."

He disappeared out the door.

"Boys. Say nothing about Castledawn. Just say we got soaked and I got lost," whispered DJ.

"Aye, but what about the noise? What about the doors slamming shut?" said James.

"I'll tell you later. Something happened. Listen, I know what's inside the sack, wrapped in chains..."

"Right boys, you OK to walk to the lochan?" Mr Mackenzie interrupted.

They nodded and put on their boots... Mr Mackenzie had put rolled up newspaper in DJ's wellies to dry them out a wee bit – they were still wet and cold. With his borrowed sweatshirt and tracksuit bottoms, at least he was warm.

Stars twinkled in the sky and there was only a faint breeze. With the haar gone and the rain off it wasn't dark. No need for a torch really, but Mr Mackenzie had brought his big Eveready spotlight, its beam illuminated the path to the water. As they neared, the bundle DJ found was caught in the torchlight.

"Oh here. What could that be?" said Mr Mackenzie.

Putting the torch on the grass he set about removing the rusty chain coiled around the sack. The boys looked on – fascinated and a wee bit scared. Chain off, he used his penknife to slice down the middle of the sack. Inside was a body – its hands and feet tied; a cloth bag covered its head. James and DJ stepped forward to look closer. John stepped back. Mr Mackenzie looked shocked and was muttering words under his breath. He gently cut the rope on the wrists and ankles, and taking a deep breath, he carefully removed the cloth hood. DJ and James took another step forward. John was frozen on the spot. The body was that of a young boy. His face was white, almost translucent, the skin, tight on his skull as if it had shrunk. His eyes, closed, but it was his hair. DJ couldn't take his eyes off his hair. The black-haired boy from his dreams. It was him. No doubt about it whatsoever.

"We'll need to be making a phone call to Uig boys. This is a job for Constable Williams." said the Coastguard. His hand was shaking in the torchlight.

"Who do you think it is?" James asked.

"Och, I don't know, laddie. By the looks of him he's been here a long time. Could've been buried in the peat and over the years with the rain the lochan has gotten bigger. Look at what he's wearing, see how well preserved he is. That's the peat. Poor wee soul."

The boys stayed with the body whilst Mr Mackenzie went to call the Police.

"It's him. From my dreams. It's the boy in the bath. It's him. I know it," said DJ.

"You sure?" said John. "Really, are you sure DJ?"

"Aye. Positive. It's him alright."

"What we going to tell the Police?" said James.

"Tell them the truth. We were out camping, and DJ got lost and fell into the lochan," replied John.

"Aye. No need to tell them about Castledawn. There's no way I'm telling them about my dreams. They'd lock me in the nuthouse. We were camping and I got lost. That's the story we stick to. OK?"

The brothers nodded. If their folks found out they'd broken into Castledawn they'd be for the high jump. There was no need for them to know.

Mr Mackenzie reappeared with a tarpaulin and covered the black-haired boy's body. He crossed his chest and said something in Gaelic. A short prayer.

"OK boys. Constable Williams is on the way. I phoned your mum again DJ, she'll come to take the three of you home. John your father knows as well. I told him DJ's mum will drop you off. Not much point in all of us hanging around here. You three go back inside. I'll wait with the wee laddie."

The boys sat in the kitchen not saying much and when the police car pulled up John reminded them to stick to the story. They went to greet Constable Williams.

"Lads. Seems you've had a bit of excitement, eh? You just stay here. I'll see Mr. Mackenzie. A couple of my colleagues from the Portree are on their way."

He walked down to the lochan and spoke to the Coastguard. Kneeling beside the body, he pulled the tarpaulin back for a brief moment and shook his head. Car lights appeared on the road, DJ's mum in the Beetle, she looked worried but smiled as she got out of the car. She took DJ in her arms and asked the brothers if they were all right.

"And how are you, darling? Must have been a bit of a shock. Were you scared?"

"A wee bit. Aye. Mr Mackenzie thinks the body's been there a long time. Thinks it might have been buried in the peat."

"So he said on the phone. Pure luck you found it. You could've been drowned DJ. Wandering about in the mist."

"Oh Mum, the water wasn't deep. Anyway, I'm a good swimmer. I'm OK... Honest."

"Shouldn't have let you go camping with the weather being so bad."

"Mum... This is Skye. We're used to it," he smiled.

She kissed his cheek and hugged him, not letting him out of her arms until Constable Williams came back up to speak to him.

"So, you got lost in the haar did you? Lucky you didn't drown," he said.

"That's what I just told him," said his mum.

DJ rolled his eyes at the boys, and the three exchanged looks.

"Mr Mackenzie right, about the body, probably been there for a long, long time. It's almost mummified."

"What will you do with him?" DJ asked.

"Well, they'll take him to Portree Hospital first and transfer him to the mortuary in Inverness later. They'll want to examine him. See what happened. Maybe they can tell us how long he's been dead for."

"So, Evan... is it alright if I take these three home? It's been quite an adventure. They all look shattered," said DJ's mum.

"Oh, aye Annie. No problem. You get away home. I'll be here until the Portree boys arrive. If I need anything I'll phone you."

"Right... You three... Car... Now."

"What about our bikes?" said DJ.

"And the tent?" added James.

'Och... Don't think you'll need to worry about anyone stealing your stuff from here. I'll ask Mr Mackenzie if he can drop them off tomorrow. If not, I'll do it," said the Constable.

DJ wasn't happy about leaving his new bike out in the elements overnight but he'd no choice. On the way home DJ and James sat in the back and John sat beside his mum. Nobody said much, all DJ could think about was his bike. After all that had happened, he was more worried about his Chopper Sprint than anything else.

When they got back to the house Maggie and Norman were there. They'd been looking after a sleeping Catriona. Maggie gave DJ a big hug. Norman ruffled his hair. Everyone was happy no harm had come to the three of them. Norman joked he'd have some story to tell the lassies in school. DJ hadn't thought about it but when he did, the only lassie he wanted to tell was Claire. Might even tell her about Castledawn.

It was after two o'clock before he got to bed and as soon as his head touched the pillow, he was out like a light.

Chapter 25

DJ woke to the sound of a car engine and the voice of Mr Mackenzie returning the Chopper. He lay for a while thinking about what had happened. There were still more questions than answers. Was it a total coincidence he got separated from the boys? The slamming doors. The bloodworm beast. Falling through the floor and what about being chased by the horse and carriage? His dad's hand pulling him from the water. Was he meant to find the black-haired boy? The dreams. Were they messages? Too many strange things had happened since they first set foot inside Castledawn house. Too many questions and not enough answers.

Getting up and dressed he winced in pain. His back hurt from the fall. Going downstairs he realised there was no black-haired boy dreams in the night. No dad. In fact, he hadn't dreamt at all.

"Morning lazybones," said his mum.

"Babybones, babybones," laughed Catriona.

"How are you feeling? Did you sleep OK?"

"Like a log."

He was about to tell her his back hurt but caught himself just in time. If he told her about how he had injured his back, he'd have to tell her everything and if he did that, she'd never let him leave Linicro again, or at least until he was eighteen!

"Mr Mackenzie dropped off your bike and your clothes. Said you could keep the clothes you borrowed. Very nice of him."

"What happened to the body?"

"The Portree Police took it to the hospital. Probably on its way to Inverness now. They'll do a post-mortem, maybe they'll find the cause of death. Mr Mackenzie reckons it was murder. The way the poor wee boy was tied up and all."

"Aye. Murder no doubt, but when? I mean... How long ago and who did it?"

"Well, Evan... Constable Williams is very knowledgeable about local history. Said he'll look through the archives in Portree, see if any kids went missing in the North End. I doubt there'll be many. Could be interesting."

"Hope there isn't a crazy child killer roaming Duntulm," DJ joked.

"Oh DJ... Don't say that. Whatever happened to that wee boy it might've been over a hundred years ago. That's what Mr Mackenzie thinks. Let's see what the police in Inverness say."

After his porridge DJ went to inspect his bike. Mr Mackenzie had parked it outside the front door. Grabbing a rag and a wee can of 3 in 1 oil he gave it a good wipe down and carefully applied globules of oil to the chain and the brakes. After, he wheeled it to the shed. Back in the house he sat having a strupag with his mum.

"Not long now till school starts darling. We need to take a trip to Portree. Get you kitted out for second year."

"Suppose," he replied.

"What? You not excited about going back? Seeing your other friends?"

"Suppose."

His mum got up to go to the kitchen, ruffling his hair as she passed.

"Don't forget about the water," she said.

"Suppose."

The rest of the day he hung around the house, playing with Catriona and helping his mum. Unusually, he'd no desire to go anywhere. He wanted to stay close to his family, and in the evening, he sat outside with Catriona. Looking down the croft to the boy's house, he wondered how they were. It'd only been one day, but he missed his pals. Norman visited and brought fresh milk, saying the news of DJ finding a body was hot gossip across Linicro.

"Maybe you'll be on the front page of the Free Press."

"Aye... I'll be famous."

"That you will boy. That you will."

"Norman, did you ever hear of children going missing. You know... Like years ago?"

"Are you saying I'm old?"

"Aren't you?" laughed DJ.

"Cheeky blighter. No, I didn't hear of such a thing. The wee laddie could've been buried in a peat bog for over a century. It preserves the body you see. The peat."

"Aye... So I've been told."

***

That night under the covers he stared at the night shadows on the wall. Thinking about his dad and how he'd came into his dreams and helped DJ find the black-haired boy. And as he slept, he had normal thirteen-year-old boy dreams. One was about Claire Ross. She was riding a carousel and waving to him, he waved back. DJ thought the guy collecting the money on the ride looked like his dad.

***

With less than two weeks of the school holidays left the Linicro tearaways wanted to make the most of their free time and DJ wanted to make the most of his new bike. They went on bike runs to Uig and across the bealach road to Staffin, way behind the Linicro rocks. One day they hung out at the River Rha and even made a trip to the Fairy Glen in Sheader. They had an unspoken agreement they wouldn't take their bikes north of Kilmuir hall. They'd seen enough of Castledawn. That place was just too strange and creepy. Still, they talked about it, though.

DJ's dreams of the boy in the bath were clues to find the body. Clues he'd missed or didn't understand. He had needed his dad to point him in the right direction. It kind of made sense. What made no sense was the bloodworm beast, doors slamming shut on their own and the horrendous smell. DJ hadn't forgotten the horse drawn carriage with the dead eyed ghoul at the reins and what about the hidden room upstairs in the bathroom. Everything that happened in Castledawn made absolutely no sense. Not yet anyway.

John, James and DJ agreed to give themselves a break from thinking about it all. Instead, they talked about being famous for finding a dead body and they wondered if there would be a reward.

Epilogue

The night before school began Constable Williams came to the house to talk to DJ and his mum. He had news about the body. An autopsy had been performed and with the help of local records in Portree he felt confident they had identified the black-haired boy. A seven-year-old called Donald Angus MacPherson who had gone missing from his house in Duntulm in 1855 and was never seen again. Constable Williams had a copy of a newspaper clipping, which DJ's mum read.

"It's just terrible. His poor parents," she said.

"Aye, that it is," said the policeman.

"Do they know how he died? Was he drowned?" asked DJ.

"The report can't confirm the exact cause of death, but he had a serious head injury and injuries to his upper body. It was suggested it could've been an accident which someone tried to cover up by hiding the body. We'll probably never know the truth."

"Such a shame," said DJ's mum.

"One curious thing I did discover, not long before he went missing two other children had disappeared."

"Really?" said DJ.

"Aye. One laddie from Earlish and another from Kensaleyre. Vanished. Not a trace. The newspaper reported they'd probably drowned at sea. It's interesting. I plan to do more research when I have time."

"Do you think the boy still has family in the area?" DJ asked.

"There's no Macpherson's in Duntulm now. The records show the family moved to the mainland, but it didn't say where."

After finishing a second cup of tea the Constable said goodnight. DJ helped his mum prepare his stuff for school. Before sleeping he read through the pages of the Pigmentarium Novis, thinking that one day he might show it to Constable Evans. He'd have to come up with a plausible story about how he found it though. He couldn't admit to breaking into a house. Not to a policeman!

***

"DJ... DJ... Wake up, son. DJ... DJ!"

DJ's eyes opened to the familiar sound.

"DJ... DJ... Are you awake?"

Getting out of bed, he opened the skylight. At the gate was his dad. Smiling.

"DJ you have to help them. You have to find them, son."

For readers who would like to find out more about the Castledawn story here is a short extract from the next book in the series: *'Anastasia Black — Baobhan Sith'*

1.

The boys first week back at Portree High was pretty funny. Their three smiling faces had been plastered on the front page of the West Highland Free Press. The story of how they found a body had been read by folk all across the island. The school bus buzzed. DJ, John and James basked in their new-found fame. Even better was the fact that DJ had had no more strange dreams. On the Friday lunch break DJ met Claire on Somerled Square. He gave her the inside scoop on their summer holiday adventure, and he walked her back to school. As the afternoon bell went, she touched his hand and asked him to meet her at Uig bakers the next day. They could go for a walk along the shore at Cuil. Flustered DJ agreed with red cheeks and as he changed into his football gear for afternoon activities all he could think about was Claire. For the rest of the afternoon, he ran around the red blaes football pitch trying to get a kick of the ball.

On the bus home he sat with James. John being older meant he sat on the backseat with his pals. There was a pecking order on the bus and the older you were, the closer you got to the backseat. DJ and James sat two rows away. It would take a couple more years for them to make it to the back.

"So, what's the plan for tonight?" James asked.

"Homework," DJ Replied. "Got plenty and I want to finish it so I have Saturday and Sunday free."

He neglected to tell the brothers about his afternoon date with Claire.

"What... You're staying in to do your homework?"

"Aye."

"Swot."

DJ elbowed James in the ribs.

"Better than trying to cram it all in on Sunday night," he smiled.

"Swot," James repeated.

***

After finishing his maths and history homework he sat with his mum and Catriona. A farming program played on the radio; DJ wished he could tune it to Radio One. His mum was reading the Oban Times and drinking her tea. Catriona was on the floor with a million coloured pencils drawing abstract art pieces in one of his old school jotters. Bess studied her work with interest. DJ's thoughts were on Uig and specifically meeting up with Claire. These thoughts made him feel nervous, not in a bad way – a good way.

"Mum, I'm going to Uig tomorrow do you need anything at the shop?"

"Don't think so darling. Got most of the stuff yesterday in Portree. Do you and the boys have something planned? Better behave yourselves."

"Eh... No...The boys are busy I'm meeting one of my friends from school."

"OK... So? Who are you meeting?"

"Just a friend. We might go to the shore for an hour or two."

"A secret friend, eh? As long as you do your chores and don't come home late."

"I'll be back before teatime. Don't worry,"

***

Under the bedclothes and with his torch on his shoulder DJ began reading The Swiss Family Robinson, a book from school and required reading in his English class. The story was about a family who got shipwrecked on a remote island and have to fend for themselves. The book fired up his imagination and transported him to the South Pacific where he joined Fritz, Ernest, Jack, and Franz on their jungle island adventure. Hidden underneath his bed in an old suitcase was the Pigmentarium Novis. Out of sight but not out of mind. DJ just didn't want to read it. Not now. The last time he dreamt of his dad was when he asked DJ to help find 'them.' Since then, he hadn't dreamt about him at all. He was glad he wasn't receiving cryptic messages anymore, but he did miss seeing his dad's face in his dreams.

***

His morning chores done, DJ wheeled out the Chopper Sprint and gave it a good wipe down. After applying 3 in 1 oil to the chain and the gear and brake cables he was raring to go to Uig.

"I'm off mum. Sure you don't need anything from the shop?"

"Don't need anything but you could treat your sister to lolliplop."

"Lolliplop. Lolliplop. Lolliplop," chanted Catriona from the living-room floor. Bess wagged her tail. Lolliplop sounded tasty to her.

The afternoon sky was grey. It could rain but knowing Skye it could clear up and be sunny. DJ was unconcerned. He'd cycle through a snow drift to see Claire Ross. Miss Murchison was at her door and waved him to stop.

"Where are you off to in such a hurry?"

"The bakers. Do you need anything?"

"Och no laddie. Got my weekly shopping from Portree. Saw your mum on Wentworth Street. DJ, I need to speak to you son. Can you pop in on your way back? I've got a Mr Kipling's almond slice waiting for you."

"Aye. No problem. I'll call in later."

"That'll be grand laddie. That'll be grand."

He pushed on up the road wondering what the old girl wanted, he hoped it would be an odd job or two as the purchase of the bike had all but wiped out his savings. What a difference having three gears made biking to the top of Totescore. Easy. From the top of Uig he bombed it to the bakers.

Passing the Uig Post Office the butterflies in his stomach were flapping like mad. Arriving at the shop there was no sign of Claire. Not at first. Peering through the window he saw her at the counter. Two Cornetto's in hand. Looked like chocolate chipped mint flavour – one of DJ's favourites. She appeared at the door and DJ was all smiles.

"Good timing," she smiled.

"Is one of them for me?"

"What...You think I'd eat two and not offer you one," she replied. Face serious.

"No...Of course not...I...," spluttered DJ.

"DJ, I'm kidding," she smiled. That Claire Ross smile. "Of course one's for you."

DJ regained some composure as he asked her to wait whilst he parked his bike at the side of the bakery. No need for a padlock and chains. They sat on the bridge across the Conon – eating their cold treat. DJ struggled to say anything of meaning and was totally unsure of what to do. Luckily, Claire did most of the talking. He was fine with that. He could sit and listen to her talk all day – no problem.

Ice cream finished they walked towards the Cuil road.

"So? Are you getting fed up with the attention yet?" she asked.

"What do you mean?"

"You know. 'The boy that found the body.' That kinda stuff,"

"Wouldn't say I'm getting all that much attention," he smiled.

"My mum said there was a wee bit about it in the Oban Times."

"Really? My mum reads that too, but she never mentioned anything."

"What was it like then...? You know... finding a dead body."

"To be honest, a relief. What with all the night...," he caught himself.

No way was he telling her about the dreams and Castledawn. She'd think he was a nutter.

"A relief?" she asked.

"Eh... what I mean is... It was a relief to find the wee boy after all these years. He could get a proper burial. That kind of thing."

"Ah... I see what you mean."

They walked the Cuil road in silence. The tide was out though not much shore was left bare by the receding water.

"Over here DJ. Here's my spot."

There was nothing remarkable about the spot. It was clear someone used it for sitting – the long grass had been flattened. It was just a grassy seat above the shore. Using their jackets as protection from wet bums, they sat down. The view of the bay was unusual at this height. The pier was almost exactly opposite. The sea didn't move much. Waves licked the shoreline. Turns out it was a pretty good spot to sit. Behind them, on the hill, was Captain Fraser's Folly, a round 19th century reproduction of a castle turret built with grey stone. Standing guard, watching over the village.

It was peaceful. DJ felt relaxed and he felt an urge. An overwhelming urge to tell Claire about Castledawn. Tell her everything, even if it did risk her thinking he was bonkers.

"Do you know Castledawn? The old house down by Score Bay, near the castle?"

"Think everybody in the North End knows that place. It's as well known as the tower behind us. What about it?"

"Well...Eh...I've got a story to tell... I mean... About Castledawn. If I tell you, will you keep it to yourself?"

"A secret? What are you talking about DJ."

"Look... I know you might think I'm a looney, but something happened...I mean a lot of stuff happened, but it all started the day me, John and James went inside Castledawn house."

"You went inside? What... Was the door opened?"

"Not exactly. If I tell you, will you keep it a secret Claire?"

"Aye. I will. Tell me."

Over the next hour he told her everything. The camping trip; breaking into Castledawn; the whispered voice; the hidden room; the book; the dreams about the black-haired boy in the bath; the dreams about his dad, he only hesitated when it came to talking about the bloodworm beast. He worried he'd scare her off home. He told though, everything. Once he started, he couldn't stop. It felt good to talk to someone other than the boys. Like a weight was lifted from his shoulders. He finished by telling her about the last dream he had – his dad asking to 'find them.' Claire listened. She looked at his face and listened to every word and said nothing until DJ had completely unburdened himself. They sat in silence. Claire broke the silence.

"That's some story. Scary too."

"You believe me? You don't think I'm a madman?" he nervously asked.

"Why wouldn't I believe you? If you said it happened, it happened."

What a lassie. Most folk would've ran a mile, but not her.

It started to rain. Only wee drops but knowing Skye they could turn into big drops. They got up and put on their jackets.

"I'll walk you to your gate. Better be getting back to Linicro before it buckets it down."

"A true gentleman," she smiled.

It was only spitting down as they reached her gate. DJ struggled with what to do. Does he kiss her? Shake her hand. Just wave goodbye... What should he do? Claire had an answer. She leaned forward and kissed his cheek.

"Thanks for sharing your story, DJ Mackay. You've given me a lot to think about. See you on Monday."

DJ couldn't speak. His brain was processing the kiss. Before going into her house Claire turned and said "Oh... and by the way... I'd never think you were a madman."

And with that she was gone.

DJ felt brilliant. He felt lighter. He couldn't wait to tell the boys that Claire Ross kissed his cheek – in front of her house! On the way back to the bakers he debated whether he should tell John and James that Claire knew everything. Hopping on his bike he headed home. The rain came on – heavy. He was soon soaked but didn't care. Claire Ross had kissed his cheek!

Well and truly drookit, DJ knocked on Miss Murchison's door.

"Hi Miss Murchison. It's me," he shouted.

"Oh, DJ laddie, you're wringing wet. Get yourself by the fire and I'll make you a wee cuppa tea."

Wet he was but he didn't feel cold. The warmth of the recent cheek kiss remained in his body. He sat at the fire opposite the old girl's corner seat. The heat made steam rise from his denims.

"There you go son. Sweet tea, just how you like it. That'll warm you," she handed him a blue and white striped mug, full to the brim.

"Brilliant. Thanks."

"And a couple of almond slices for the growing laddie."

With her cup in hand, she sat in her chair.

"So, DJ. You'll be wondering what I want to speak to you about. Eh?"

"Are you needing something done? I can come anytime. Even after school."

"Oh laddie. There's plenty jobs needing done here right enough but that's not what I want to talk to you about."

"OK... What's up?"

"DJ, I spoke with your dad."

DJ was swallowing a bite of cake. It nearly stuck in his throat.

"Eh? What do you mean?"

"Oh, DJ laddie. Oh DJ. I've got a few things I need to tell you and I don't want you to be frightened."

"Frightened?"

"Aye. I know more about Castledawn than I told you, son. I know a lot more."

"Really? What?"

"Are you ready for a bit of a story?"

"Aye... Go on then."

DJ's mind was turning. She had spoken to his dad? She knows about Castledawn? Maybe the old girl's losing her marbles.

"Remember I told you my people were from Greulin? Well, they weren't just any family. Back then my mother and grandmother were known to be different. They called them Ban-Fhiosaiche. They had gifts. Do you know what a fortune teller is DJ?"

"Aye. Someone who can see into the future or something."

"Well...My mother was a cailleach who had the gift. She could see things. Things other people couldn't see. She could talk to folk on the other side."

"The other side of what?"

"The spirits laddie. She could talk to the departed,"

"You mean dead people?"

"Aye. That I do laddie. That I do."

What the heck? Why was she telling him this now? What did his dad talk to her about?

"You said you spoke to my dad?"

"Oh aye. I did. He came to me in a dream?"

"Really? A dream?"

"He did."

"What did he say?"

"He had a message for you son. Maybe it was a message for both of us."

"What did he say?"

"He told me he was very proud of you. How brave you were to find the wee boy in the lochan. You see, the wee boy's spirit was stuck here in the material world. He couldn't move on. You finding his body released him to carry on his spiritual journey."

"Spiritual journey?" repeated DJ. Maybe she had lost her marbles after all.

"Aye son. Comes to us all. Your dad too. That was his message. He had to move on. Told me to tell you and that he loves you so much. Told me to tell you to 'find them.'

DJ's head was spinning. What the actual heck. Find who?

"You see DJ, I've got my mother's gift too. The Ban-Fhiosaiche * is passed from mother to daughter. It's why I never married. Some of us don't consider it a gift. Some of us think it's a curse."

DJ was still trying to wrap his mind around what the old lady was saying.

"That's not all son. It's Castledawn."

"What...Castledawn...What do you mean?"

"Och, I don't what to frighten you laddie, but I know you've seen what lies within its walls. What still lives there. In the cellar."

How the heck does she know all this?

"Son, the Ban-Fhiosaiche are more than just fortune tellers. We're soothsayers, healers. Some folk call us charmers. We live in two worlds."

"Two worlds?"

"Aye. This world and the world of the Daoine Sith. The Otherworld."

"The other world," DJ's wee head was about to implode.

"Aye boy. I know it's a lot to take in. I won't overburden you son. You've been through a lot over the last few years. What with your dad and all. What with Castledawn. It's just...There's some things you need to know... To keep you and your family safe."

---

* Ban-Fhiosaiche – a soothsayer, fortune teller or prophetess.

"My family? My mum doesn't know anything about what happened at Castledawn, and I'd like to keep it that way."

"I know son. I know. And I'm here to help you. I might be old but I'm hardy and my mind is as clear now as it was when I worked at Castledawn."

"What else is there? What about Castledawn?"

"Well... I didn't go to Castledawn because I wanted to be a housekeeper. I went there because I got a message from the Daoine Sith."

"A message?"

"Aye. I went there to protect Monty. The wee boy I told you about."

"Protect him? Protect him from what?"

"Not from what. From whom son. From whom. I think you saw her. Well at least a version of her?"

"I didn't see anyone. Not really. Maybe in a dream."

"But you saw something in Castledawn didn't you?"

"Aye. I think I did. It wasn't a woman. It was a beast... it seemed to be made up of bloodworms... a bloodworm beast."

"It was Anastasia Black you saw. I saw her too. She's the reason I was there. To protect young Monty from her."

"I don't understand Miss Murchison. Who's Anastasia Black?"

"She was the wife of Cornelius Black. The original owner of Castledawn. She wanted young Monty. I was there to protect him from her, DJ. I know it's a lot to take in, but you need to know what we're up against. Anastasia is no ordinary woman. She's alive but she's dead too."

"I'm not sure I follow you. Alive and dead?"

"Aye boy. Exactly. Anastasia's a Baobhan Sith*. A black witch. A sanguimancer. A shapeshifter."

"A what?"

"Son, there's light and dark in the Daoine Sith. Ban-Fhiosaiche are light. Baobhan Sith are dark."

"You mean like...Good and evil?"

"That I do boy. That I do."

"What's it all got to do with me Miss Murchison? I'm not a fortune teller or healer. I'm just a kid from Edinburgh."

"Anastasia, DJ. Anastasia wants you. She needs you. Your life-force son. Your very essence. She won't stop. She can't stop. I couldn't save Monty back then, I was too young. I didn't understand the danger, thought I did and look what happened to him."

"You told me he died of an asthma attack or something. In his parent's bathroom."

"Aye that I did. That's the story most folk round here know but it's not the truth DJ. It was Anastasia who killed, drained him of life and now she's after you."

"What are we going do?" said a visibly shaken DJ.

"Laddie. We need to go back to Castledawn."

***

When he got back to the house, DJ was in a total daze. Late for dinner, his mum gave him what for. He told her Miss Murchison wanted him to do a few odd jobs and she'd kept him there talking. Said he felt sorry for

---

* A banshee, a mystical creature who took the form of a beautiful woman and liked to drink blood.

the old lady – she seemed lonely. Feeling guilty, his mum kissed his cheek and heated up his dinner. In bed, he couldn't read his Sparky. Couldn't concentrate. Everything Miss Murchison said played and replayed in his head. Basically, she was a witch but a good witch. A white witch. There was more too. She told him he'd need to bring the boys to her. John and James were in danger. They protected DJ and Anastasia is threatened by them. How the heck was he going to explain everything Miss Murchison had told him? He could see the looks on their faces. They'd think he and the old lady were stark raving mad. But he'd promised her. And what about the book under his bed? And *who* the heck was the 'them' he had to find?

A Baobhan Sith? DJ didn't like the sound of that. A shapeshifter? Not good, he thought. And what the bloody hell was a sanguimancer?

www.ingramcontent.com/pod-product-compliance
Lightning Source LLC
LaVergne TN
LVHW051216070526
838200LV00063B/4919